Cosmos' Promise:
Cosmos' Gateway Book 4

By S.E. Smith

Acknowledgments
I would like to thank my husband Steve for believing in me and being proud enough of me to give me the courage to follow my dream. I would also like to give a special thank you to my sister and best friend Linda, who not only encouraged me to write but who also read the manuscript. Also to my other friends who believe in me: Julie, Jackie, Lisa, Sally and Narelle. The girls that keep me going!
—S.E. Smith

Montana Publishing
Science Fiction Romance
COSMOS' PROMISE: COSMOS' GATEWAY BOOK 4
Copyright © 2013 by Susan E. Smith
First E-Book Publication July 2013
Cover Design by Melody Simmons

Summary: Cosmos's latest experiment has opened a gateway into a whole new world, and the inhabitants of that world are turning his life upside down, especially one aggravating alien female.

ISBN: 978-1-942562-46-7 (paperback)
ISBN: 978-1-942562-10-8 (eBook)

Published in the United States by Montana Publishing.

{1. Science Fiction Romance – Fiction. 2. Science Fiction – Fiction. 3. Paranormal – Fiction. 4. Romance – Fiction.}

www.montanapublishinghouse.com

Synopsis

Cosmos Raines is considered to be one of the most brilliant inventors in the world. A prodigy, he is a self-made billionaire who would rather be in his lab than jet-setting around the world. Things change when his latest experiment literally opens a Gateway into a whole new world. Now, not only has his best friend and her family moved to a new star system through the Gateway he has opened, but he finds himself with a warehouse full of alien guests, including one very aggravating female that has turned him inside out.

Terra 'Tag Krell Manok has spent her life in the shadows of her three older brothers. Her home world of Baade is a male dominated world where females are few in numbers and protected to the point of captivity. Terra's father is the high chancellor of the Prime and considered to be the fiercest warrior of their world next to her brothers. No one defies him and lives. Terra is surprised when her father suddenly sends her through the Gateway into hiding to protect her from a clan insisting that she be mated for political purposes. The last thing she expects to find there is her bond mate - in the form of a human male!

Cosmos may not have been expecting to find the woman of his dreams on the other side of the Gateway he built, but he knows one thing for sure - no one is going to take her away from him - not the clan who wants to use her nor her father who thinks all human males are worthless.

When she is taken from him, he will use every bit of his intelligence and ingenuity to not only track her down, but steal her back. He will prove that human males can be just as much a warrior as a Prime one, especially when it involves the woman he loves.

Contents

Chapter 1

"RITA, run those numbers again for me and send it to my tablet," Cosmos said distractedly as he reached up for the cup of coffee he had set on top of the file cabinet.

He took a huge gulp before he grimaced. It was not only ice cold, it tasted like shit. He must have forgotten to make a new batch last night - or was it this morning? He gave a blurry-eyed look at the watch on his wrist before he gave a command for it to just tell him the time. His eyes were so tired he couldn't even read the damn thing anymore.

"RITA, on second thought, just tell me what it says," Cosmos called out to the computer system he and Tilly Bell, the mom of his best friend, Tink, had designed.

Well, he had designed the super-computer, but Tilly had hacked into it one weekend when she was visiting her youngest daughter, Jasmine 'Tinker' Bell. Tilly had uploaded into his NOVAD computer system an experimental artificial intelligence program she had designed.

The program named RITA soon took over his entire system, learning and developing at an exponential rate to the point he just thought of it as another pain in his ass when she gave him attitude. RITA stood for Really Intelligent Technical Assistant. Cosmos had called her a few other things. After taking cold showers for almost a month in the middle of a Maine winter, he had learned to keep his less than ideal thoughts to himself.

Tink's parents, Tilly and Angus Bell, had practically adopted him when he and Tink met a little over four years ago while they were all camping at a campground not far from Calais, Maine. He and Tink had clicked, their minds and personalities made for the perfect balance of acceptance and respect. While he had hoped at one point that it might develop into something else, he realized that he would always see Tink as the little sister he never had. She had become not only the sister figure, but his best friend.

He found he could talk to her about anything. Her knowledge and ingenuity with motors and power generators blew him away and she loved to listen to his newest crazy ideas. When Tilly and Angus decided to move on when Tink was eighteen, she decided to stay. She moved into the third floor of the warehouse and a comfortable companionship had developed.

All of that changed a few months back when he needed help with his current project – a Gateway portal. He had been working on opening a doorway between two places on Earth, not two places between star systems!

He had asked Tink to work on the generators. He needed more power. He had planned to be there, but was called away to Chicago to meet up with his parents.

A shudder went through him as he remembered that morning when he arrived back unexpectedly. Fortunately for Tink and him, his parents cancelled out on him at the last minute. He didn't even want to think what could have happened if they hadn't.

Hell, he thought, *who am I kidding? Look at what still happened!*

The Gateway had been a huge success, at least from a scientific viewpoint. From a personal one, it was a disaster! His once quiet home was now crawling with aliens from another world.

Correction, Prime Warriors from Baade, he silently corrected himself.

Now, one of them was missing, two of them were out there somewhere looking for their 'mates' and another one was about to drive him out of his mind. The male that was missing and the two warriors running loose he could handle. The female who was currently sleeping in Tink's former bedroom was totally another matter. He briefly closed his eyes and breathed deeply, trying to drive the image of the beautiful alien female out of his mind. None of the techniques he used to help him remain focused were working – at least not with her.

Grumbling under his breath, Cosmos walked over to the small kitchenette area he had built into his lab and poured the remaining brew of coffee down the drain. He didn't care what anyone said, Cowboy Coffee tasted like shit. He quickly made another pot, breathing in the fragrant aroma as it ground the fresh Kopi Luwak beans he special ordered. He didn't give a damn about the origin of the beans, it was the jolt from these particular beans that he needed to stay alert.

I definitely need to be alert now that my latest project is a success, he thought wearily.

"Cosmos dear," RITA's voice hummed out in a voice that was an exact duplicate of Tilly Bell's husky tones. "Your guest is awake."

Cosmos bit back a curse and looked down at his left palm. In the center of it was a series of intricate circles. The damn things pulsed with life, pulling a smothered groan of pain from him as his body reacted to it. A wave of heat flooded him, rolling over his hypersensitive flesh until a light film of sweat coated his body as he fought against reacting to it. It was almost like she was stroking his skin with her long, delicate fingers.

What the hell have I gotten myself into? Cosmos muttered through clenched teeth as he felt her running her fingers over and over the mark.

His head fell forward and he tried to breath in deep, calming breaths to fight the reaction his body was having to her gentle strokes, but his damn cock was too busy pulsing to listen to him. With a loud curse, he pulled away from the counter and strode toward the doors leading out of his lab. He called out a short command to RITA to open them, bypassing the keypad. There was no way in hell he would have been able to push the damn buttons to exit the lab with the way his hands were shaking.

Who the hell needs to push buttons when they have an alien female doing it? He thought savagely. *The aggravating female upstairs is doing enough of it to last me a lifetime.* His whole body was trembling now with suppressed hunger, all thought of fatigue disappearing as the urgent need to claim the female upstairs took over.

Cosmos strode through the heavy metal doors that opened and took the stairs leading up to the second floor of the converted warehouse two at a time. He had purchased the old warehouse along the river when he was eighteen and spent millions upgrading and securing it. It had become his main living and research center.

At almost twenty-seven, he was a multi-billionaire in his own right. His defense and security systems made up almost fifty percent of his inventions, but his other inventions and systems' developments in the medical, environmental, and space research fields made up the rest. Both of his parents were world-renowned scientists, though he seldom saw them. They were currently in Asia working on different projects.

"RITA, where is she?" Cosmos gritted out as he reached the top of the stairs leading into his living quarters. His eyes flashed to the set of stairs leading up to the third floor that used to belong to Tink.

"Cosmos," a soft, startled voice said. "Is something wrong?"

Cosmos' eyes drank in the slender figure of the female hesitating on the bottom step. She was absent-mindedly stroking the palm of her left hand. Each delicate stroke caused the flames burning inside him to burst even hotter. Like a moth drawn to a light, Cosmos jerked forward, closing the space between him and the dark-haired beauty looking at him in innocent confusion.

"Yes, damn you. There is something wrong," he said hoarsely when he slid his large hands around her smaller ones in an effort to get her to stop the torture she was inflicting.

"What....?"

Cosmos didn't give the beautiful, silver-eyed female a chance to say another word. His lips crushed hers in a savage, burning kiss. His hands let go of hers as he slid them around her narrow waist, pulling her closer to his throbbing length.

"Terra," he groaned softly. "You are killing me with your touch. I promised your brother I would protect you with my life, but I swear if you don't stop, I'll take you right here and now."

Terra 'Tag Krell Manok's soft gasp died on her lips as Cosmos once again claimed them with his own. Her body melted into his as his fingers gently kneaded her hips. Her hands slowly crept up until she could bury them in the silky brown strands of hair touching the back of his collar, pulling him even closer.

How could I have ever thought of human males as being weak? She wondered vaguely as his strong arms pulled her close.

* * *

Cosmos was lost in the sensations coursing through his body. Everything in him was focused on the slender female standing in the circle of his arms. She was only a couple of inches shorter than his six feet two inches. Her long black hair hung down her back like a silky waterfall. The temptation to wind it around his fingers so he could hold her to him was too tempting to resist. He shuddered as her hands rose up to grasp his broad shoulders, her fingernails curling into his hard flesh before moving to entwine with his shaggy hair.

A soft moan escaped him as he pulled back far enough to gaze down into her dark silver eyes. His hazel eyes glittered with frustration, annoyance, and desire as unfamiliar emotions crashed through the defenses he had carefully erected over a lifetime of being different.

He had created a very elaborate picture of himself to the outer world. While considered a bit of a playboy nerd to those who read the newspapers, gossip magazines, and tabloids, he was just the opposite. He might have been born with a silver spoon in his mouth, but it didn't show.

His parents had made a mint off of the different patents they had developed and he was just like them in that regard. He had also earned his doctorate by the time he was twenty-two. He modified the warehouse he was living in near the river and designed it as a combination lab/home so he would have a nondescript place to live that would draw little attention as he followed his true passion.

The image he created fit in with what he wanted the world to believe. Even Tink, his best friend and former roommate, was unaware of ninety percent of what he did. It was safer for her, or it had been before she got swept off her feet by a huge Prime warrior from Baade.

He used the carefully conceived misconception of Cosmos Raines to hide the work he did. He had begun building the outer shell he needed as a cover when he was sixteen. Now, his billion dollar companies were run by some of the smartest, deadliest men and women in the world.

He had carefully selected each of them with the help of RITA over the past six years. His desire to make a difference in the world had not come from comic book heroes, but from seeing the damage being done through his own experiences. He had been the target of kidnappers since he was little more than a toddler. First, by governments and madmen around the world who wanted to use his parents, then later because of his own abilities. He had surpassed his parents long ago.

News and academic institutions claimed he was smarter than Einstein. Cosmos could care less if he was or not. He only knew he had been given a special gift that he planned to use for good. He was careful about the military contracts he approved.

He had a top notch group of men and women overseeing that division of his corporation. Each and every one of them owed him for their life or the life of a loved one. He never asked for payment, those that he helped out volunteered. Most he accepted, a few he had declined based on the information he had about them. He swore them to loyalty and confidentiality. In return, they would never have to worry about their financial security ever again.

Cosmos pulled in a deep breath as he felt the soft hands caressing his neck. "We....," he began before closing his eyes in frustration when he was interrupted by the only person in the world he swore was smarter than even him.

"Oh good, you're out of your hole," a cheerful voice chirped out in a voice way too full of merriment. "Morning, Terra, sweetheart. Did you sleep well?" The voice asked with a slightly amused tone that pulled on Cosmos' last nerve.

Terra took a step back from Cosmos and let her hands drop to her sides before she turned to look at the tiny figure with an amused smile of her own. "Pleasant morning to you, Tilly. Is Angus awake?"

"Oh heavens, yes. He should be back from his walk any minute now. How about I fix us some breakfast? Angus loves a good breakfast in the morning. He says it gives him the energy to make it through a day with me," Tilly said with a knowing grin. "Cosmos, go take a shower, dear. You look like you have been up all night."

Cosmos opened his eyes and glared at Tilly with a dark frown. "I have been. I got home late and had some work to do in the lab. We had a slight problem last night. What the hell are you and Angus doing here? I thought you were on Baade still," he growled out before flushing when Tilly raised her eyebrow at him. "Sorry," he muttered, running his hand over the back of his neck. He glanced at Terra's pale cheeks. "Your family is fine," he assured her hesitantly when she looked at him with worry reflected in her eyes.

Tilly came over and placed her hand on his arm. "We were. I wanted to be here to hear about what happened. No one was telling us anything back on Baade. Go take your shower," she urged gently. "I'll fix us something to eat and you can tell us what happened when you get out. Angus will be back by then," she added before turning and heading toward the small kitchen area.

Cosmos watched as Tilly disappeared into the kitchen. He turned and started walking across the spacious living area. He paused at the entrance to the hallway leading to his bedroom. He turned slightly and looked at Terra who was standing in the same spot, staring down at her left hand. With a muttered oath, he walked back to her.

Gently reaching out, he cupped her hand in his and ran his thumb over the intricate circles that were visible on her palm. He looked down at it for a moment before he cupped her lowered chin in his other hand and tilted it until she was forced to look at him. He smiled down at her before he brushed a light kiss across her lips.

"Everything will be alright," he promised her.

She smiled up at him with a smile that reflected her uncertainty. "I know," she whispered. "Go get refreshed. I will help Tilly with the morning meal."

Cosmos nodded again before he turned and strode back down the hallway. His mind was going in a hundred different directions. He both appreciated and hated when it did that. It was as if all his nerve-endings were trying to work at the same time and information was being processed in exponential amounts. He really needed to lay off the caffeine. It never helped, especially when he was exhausted.

Chapter 2

Cosmos ripped the black T-shirt off over his head, balling it up and tossing it toward the hamper in the corner as he entered his room. His muscles rippled as he rolled his shoulders, the long scar across his back stretching as he rolled them forward. The scar on his side pulled, showing a long white line as he twisted around to kick off his shoes.

He bent and pulled off his socks before he reached for the buttons on his black cargo pants. He pushed them and his boxers down. Stepping out of one leg, he caught the other leg with his foot and pulled it off before tossing them in the hamper behind his shirt. His body was taut from the workout last night and lack of sleep. Their mission had been successful, but not without casualties. He felt each one personally. The men that were wounded or killed were a part of his responsibility. It didn't matter that they had volunteered, he still felt responsible.

Cosmos gave the command for the shower to start at the pre-programmed temperature he liked. He ran his hand over his jaw. He wouldn't bother shaving. He had a light coating of whiskers, but he was too damn exhausted to worry about it. Stepping under the hot spray, he stretched his arms above his head, resting them on the tiled surface, and let the water fall over his tired body. His mind replayed every move that the teams made last night.

He had coordinated a mission to cover Tansy Bell, Tilly and Angus Bell's middle daughter, who was a government operative. The mission that had covered half a world, from Russia to the United States, had culminated late last night at the Canadian Ambassador's house.

Tansy and her Russian counterparts were supposed to target Craig Knapp, the Senior Director for the Collaborative Partnership against Terrorism, or CPAT. This was the group Tansy had belonged to before she found out they set her up to be killed. If that wasn't bad enough, she had a Russian billionaire named Boris Avilov hunting her as well. It turned out Craig Knapp was lining his pocket with Avilov's cash. Tansy found that out almost too late. If not for the help of a huge Prime warrior named Mak, she would have been dead.

Cosmos had RITA relay the information that Tansy had recovered from Avilov to his computer system so he could review the data she had stolen. In it were the details of the planned assassination of the President of the United States, Askew Thomas. What was not surprising to Cosmos was the fact that the Vice-President was working with Avilov and others, including Knapp, to see that it happened. The Vice President had his own agenda and it was not remaining in the political shadow of Thomas.

Unfortunately, Tansy, having the stubborn-headed, independent soul that was the makeup of the Bell females, was exposed by one of her former operatives who recognized her, even though she was in disguise. Now, he was missing one Prime warrior and another two who were searching for the Russian females, Natasha and Helene Baskov, who were kidnapped at the same time as Tansy. The only good thing that had come out of last night was that Craig Knapp would soon be a dead man and Mak had taken Tansy back to his world to be healed. Cosmos just hoped he kept her ass there.

He had been having RITA run the license plate numbers on every vehicle that drove through the intersections near the Canadian Ambassador's house. Every surveillance camera in the region had been uploaded to RITA who was enhancing and examining every clue available to help locate the women and Merrick, the huge Prime warrior who seemed to have disappeared into thin air with them.

"Cosmos?" Tilly's voice called from his bedroom. "If you don't get a move on, I'm sending Terra in to help get you out of there!" She threatened.

Cosmos groaned as he quickly ordered the shower off. "I'll be out in just a minute," he yelled out.

"My goodness, where did you get that scar from? That looks like a new one," Tilly said from the bathroom door.

"Jesus, Tilly!" Cosmos yelped out as he kept his body turned. Hopefully, the glass was fogged up enough from the heat of the shower so maybe she couldn't see too much. "Will you get out?" He choked back in embarrassment.

Tilly's husky laugh echoed in the spacious room, but he could tell she had turned. "It isn't like I've never seen a naked man before," she chuckled. "You should see Angus. I swear that man can…." Her voice thankfully faded as she walked away.

Cosmos' head dropped forward as he shook his head. "Only Tilly Bell can make me feel like a twelve year old again," he muttered with a chuckle. "And the last thing I need right now is to think of what Angus looks like naked," he added with a shudder as he opened the glass door and reached for a towel.

"Oh!" A startled voice gasped.

Cosmos' head jerked around at the gasp. He closed his eyes as he felt his cock react to the presence standing in his bathroom. He knew there would be no hiding his erection, even with the towel he had in front of him. He reluctantly opened his eyes to stare at the silver ones that were gazing at him with a combination of shy curiosity, wonder, and desire. A small part of him was a little annoyed that he was the only one feeling a little self-conscious right now.

"Let me guess," he said dryly. "Tilly?"

Terra nodded, reluctantly raising her eyes to meet his. "You are built very similar to the Prime males," she observed as her eyes followed a droplet of water as it ran down his chest. "You are paler and have more hair on your chest," she murmured as her eyes continued to follow the drop of water as it coursed its way further down. She drew in a sharp breath and took a step forward. "What happened to you?" She demanded when she saw a jagged scar on his hip.

Cosmos jerked back a step as she came closer. If his self-control was hanging by a thread earlier, it was non-existent now. At least, it was until her words hit him like a MACK truck. A dark frown crossed his face and his fist clenched on the towel.

"What the hell do you mean 'I'm built similar to Prime males'?" He asked darkly. "Just how many have you known?"

Terra's hand stilled as she reached out to touch the jagged scar. She looked up at him with a raised eyebrow that was so damn like Tilly's he could feel the heat rushing to his cheeks. What the hell was wrong with him? This was worse than hitting puberty in the middle of a Physics conference with nothing but a bunch of old people and a copy of Playboy to keep you sane.

Terra pulled back and crossed her arms in front of her. "I'm a healer for my people," she stated in a frosty tone. "It was part of my training to observe the physical attributes of the male body. How many I have known is none of your business unless you are willing to answer the same question! Just how many females have *you* known?" She snapped back.

Cosmos didn't think his face could get any hotter. "I shouldn't have said that," he admitted, looking away for a moment. "Ah, hell!" He muttered with a shake of his head.

A husky chuckle escaped him when he realized he was standing there holding a towel in front of him in the hopes of retaining a slight semblance of modesty for Terra. What he had forgotten was that his bathroom walls were mostly mirrors. Between the ones behind him and the ones to the side, Terra was getting almost a full view. With a shrug of his broad shoulders, he continued to wipe the water from his chest and hair before moving lower.

"What are you doing?" Terra asked in a choked voice as her eyes followed the towel. "Where did you get all those scars from?"

Cosmos' lips tightened. He didn't need to look in a mirror to know what she was seeing. He had scars from bullets, knives, and more than one explosion marring his tanned skin. He had grown accustomed to them. He wasn't actively participating in as many missions as he used to, only the ones that were personal, or were a huge risk for his men, those he still oversaw.

"I need to get dressed or Tilly will be back in here," Cosmos said, tossing the towel to one side and brushing by her. "The last thing I need is for her to launch into a description of Angus in the buff again," he said gruffly.

Terra's eyes followed Cosmos. He was a breathtaking male. The muscles in his shoulders were deceptively hidden in the clothes he wore. His back contained at least five separate scars that she knew had not only been painful, but must have come close to killing him. She had learned much from RITA over the past several months to gain a better understanding of the human anatomy in order to help Jasmine 'Tinker' Bell and her sister, Hannah, with their pregnancies.

A swell of heat rushed through her as he bent over and pulled a pair of tight, black boxers up over his taut buttocks. She felt her nipples harden with desire as she watched him dress. Everything inside her wanted to walk over and pull his clothing back off, throw him on his bed, and take possession of him. Her eyes widened in shock at the primitive, almost savage, need that was washing over her. She was confused by it. She had always been under the impression that the females of her race did not care for such physical contact, yet she was burning with a need that was about to drive her out of control. She remembered her mother talking recently about her feelings for their father. They hadn't really discussed anything in detail. While she had been curious as to her mother's recent behavior, the idea of discussing her mother and father's sexual habits made her feel – uncomfortable for some reason. The curiosity had become so overwhelming that she had finally broken down and asked Tink and Tilly about it. She had even watched the vidcom that had been recorded of Tink on her brother J'kar's warship. She had been giving the warriors instruction on something called 'oral' sex.

"Will you perform oral sex on me?" She asked out loud before she realized what she was saying.

"Will I what....?!" Cosmos choked out, right before falling face first onto the floor with a loud thud when his foot got tangled up in his pant leg as he was putting it through.

"Oh Cosmos, are you hurt?" Terra asked, rushing forward to where he was lying on the floor, his pants caught around his ankles. She knelt beside him and tried to gently roll him over so she could check to see if he had a head injury. "Cosmos?"

"Oh dear!" Tilly exclaimed from the doorway. "What happened? Is he alright?" She asked, rushing forward. "ANGUS! We need you, sweetheart! Cosmos has fainted."

* * *

Cosmos lay perfectly still and tried to breathe deeply to calm his racing mind. A part of him was wishing he could have invented a time machine so he could go back and warn his other self *not* to create the damn Gateway. The other part couldn't help but see the humor of the situation. At twenty-seven, he was, for the first time, totally unprepared for what was happening in his life.

Cosmos let Terra roll him over onto his back. He stared up into her confused and worried eyes for a moment before he placed both of his palms on her cheeks and pulled her down, giving her a hard, possessive kiss that left her sprawled across his chest. He continued to kiss her until he was sure he could say something without making a total ass of himself.

"Well, it looks like Terra has the situation under control," Angus said from the doorway. "Mm, Tilly sweetheart, you wouldn't be feeling a little faint yourself would you, darling? I think you might need a little mouth to mouth yourself," he added with a low growl.

"Oh Angus," Tilly giggled. "I was just telling Cosmos that you still turn me on when you...."

Cosmos broke off the kiss with a loud groan. "Enough! I don't want a picture of Angus nude stuck in my head!" He bit out before turning to glare up at

Angus who was chuckling. "You need to have a talk with your wife about walking into other men's bathrooms when they are in the shower," he growled out.

Angus pulled a blushing Tilly into his arms and bent her over it. "It wouldn't do any good," Angus laughed. "She would just distract me and we'd end up making love. Isn't that right, honey?"

"You better believe it, big guy," Tilly whispered staring up at Angus with a soft expression. "How you can still make my heart go crazy after all these years will always amaze me," she admitted with a deep sigh of contentment.

Angus brushed a kiss across his wife's lips before pulling her back up so she could stand next to him. He looked at Cosmos with a grin before shrugging his shoulders. Tilly was the light of his life and he wasn't ashamed to show it.

"Breakfast is getting cold," Angus said. "I'd like to eat before we get any more interruptions. I don't know about you kids, but I'm starving," he added, turning Tilly around and gently pushing her out of the room.

Cosmos looked back up at Terra who was watching with wide eyes as Angus slapped Tilly lightly on the ass as they exited the room. Both of them could hear the giggles and low murmurs as the two older Bells headed back toward the kitchen. Cosmos waited until Terra looked back down at him with a bemused expression on her face.

"Yes," he responded as her mouth opened. "They have always been like that since the day I met them and from what Tink says, all her life."

"Oh," Terra said before she pushed up on his chest so she could sit back. She watched as he sat up and pulled his pants up to his knees before he stood and pulled them the rest of the way up. "Will you?"

"Will I what?" Cosmos said as he fastened his pants.

He reached for a dark blue button-up shirt hanging on the peg near the door. He shrugged it on and began buttoning before looking at her when she didn't reply at first. She was watching his fingers as they moved down the row of buttons.

"Perform oral sex on me?" Terra asked hesitantly from where she was still kneeling on the light bamboo-covered floor.

Cosmos looked down into her inquiring eyes. A chuckle burst from his lips as he bent down and grabbed her hands to pull her up. Once she was standing in front of him, he gripped her by the hips and pulled her against his hard length, showing her how much he was reacting to her closeness.

"With pleasure," Cosmos murmured before he turned her toward the door and the direction of the kitchen. "With total pleasure," he repeated as he smacked her on the ass as she walked through the door, drawing a startled squeak from her.

Chapter 3

"Can you pass the eggs?" Angus asked as he reached for a couple of slices of whole wheat toast.

Tilly reached over and handed the bowl of scrambled eggs to Angus. She pulled a couple of pieces of toast onto her plate and spread strawberry jam on them. She waited until everyone had a full plate before she broached the subject of last night.

"Cosmos," Tilly began quietly. "Tell us what happened. Is Tansy....?" Her voice faded as fear blossomed.

Angus reached over and squeezed her hand. Both of the older Bells were worried about their middle daughter. Tansy thought she kept what she did a secret from them, but Tilly had been following her daughter's activities for years. She knew that Tansy had to deal with her own ghosts, some of which scared Tilly half to death. She couldn't help but be proud of her daughter's work trying to make the world a better/safer place to live, but she also couldn't help but wish someone else would do it now. She wasn't sure how much longer she could pretend that she was ignorant of the danger her daughter was constantly in.

Cosmos looked up from where he was pouring coffee into his cup from the carafe that Terra had placed on the table in front of him. He looked down at his cup as he thought of how much information to give her. He didn't want her to worry, but he also knew there were other dangers and that he was going to have to explain.

He set the carafe down and picked up his cup before looking at the woman who had been as much of a mother to him as his own. "Tansy will be fine. I received information that Mak was able to rescue her and has returned to his world with her." He watched as Tilly and Angus both glanced at each other with relieved sighs before he continued. "She was injured, though. The last report I received was that she was still unconscious, but the healers on Baade felt it was due more to exhaustion than the physical injuries that have already been taken care of."

Tilly just nodded, unable to respond. "Thank you, Cosmos. For everything," Angus said for the both of them.

Cosmos shrugged off the compliment, uncomfortable with the praise. "There are still others out there that need to be brought home safely and I lost two good men last night," he said, picking at the food on his plate.

"Which men?" Terra asked, folding her hands in her lap as she waited in fear. "Derik…. My father?"

Cosmos shook his head. "No, they are safe, though Derik didn't return for a few hours. I haven't had a chance to find out exactly what happened at the warehouse where Tansy was taken. Two of my men were killed last night in one of the fire fights. One had a sister and mother, and the other didn't have any family. I have accounts set up to take care of surviving family members should something like this happen. Merrick has disappeared. He went after some of the men who were shooting at us. Rico had some of his men retrace Merrick's path, but all they found were the dead bodies of the men who'd tried to kill the team members. It is as if he disappeared into thin air," Cosmos said. "I have RITA reviewing every surveillance camera in the area for information. In addition, both Natasha and Helene are still missing as well. I have Garrett working with Rico, Lan, and Brock to locate them. RITA was able to get the tag of at least one of the vehicles and possibly the other."

"I have already relayed the information to the teams," RITA responded in a cheerful voice. "You might want to eat a little faster, guys. Your company is coming up the street."

Cosmos froze in the process of taking a drink of his quickly cooling coffee. "What do you mean, company?" He growled tensely.

"I was following the transmissions and decided it might be prudent to keep an eye on any new traffic coming into Calais. It would appear Mr. Avilov might want to disappear but he isn't above sending a few of his men to visit. Can you imagine? He actually thinks to harm Tansy's family, and kill you as well, from the communications I intercepted," RITA chuckled.

Cosmos pushed away from the table, standing up and leaning forward with his hands splayed on the smooth surface. "How many and how long have you known they were in town?" Cosmos bit out in aggravation to RITA.

"Oh, she told me about an hour ago but she said we should have time for you to get a shower and eat something," Tilly replied as she quickly stuffed a piece of toast into her mouth and shooed Terra to hurry as well. "Angus needed to eat if he was going to be fighting for our lives. He gets low blood sugar and that is never good," she added as she scooped up a forkful of eggs.

Cosmos looked across the table at Tilly in disbelief. "You knew about this and didn't tell me?" He demanded as he straightened up and glared at her.

Tilly waved her fork at his plate. "Of course," she admonished. "What good would worrying about it have done? They were going to come anyway. Now, eat something. You'll feel better if you have something in your stomach."

"Tilly….," Cosmos began before he growled out in frustration. "Forget it. RITA, code Red," he called out as he moved away from the small kitchen area and toward the living room. "Show targets on the screen. I need numbers, positions, and weapons description. NOW!" He stated as he stopped in front of the couch in the living area.

Panels on the wall rose to reveal additional screens mounted into the surface. Soon, an entire wall of images showed different sections of the small town and the area around the warehouse. Six SUV's were pulling up further down the street. Cosmos cursed loudly. Avilov had no respect for life, and that included the lives of innocent people. They would be considered collateral damage as far as the billionaire was concerned.

"How many?" Cosmos asked tersely as Terra, Tilly, and Angus came to stand next to him.

"Thirteen," RITA responded. "I guess they aren't a superstitious lot."

Cosmos ignored RITA's ridiculous comment. His mind was already working on the different ways to contain what was about to happen. He didn't want to involve the local law enforcement but if there were going to be dead bodies he might not have much of a choice. Still, he needed to minimize the possibility of an innocent bystander getting hurt.

"Angus," Cosmos said, still watching the screens as the figures began moving up along the sides and back of the warehouse. Two split off and turned the corner coming around to the front of the warehouse. "I need you three to head to the lab, use the back elevator. I want you to take the women back to Baade. RITA, unlock the front, side, and back doors once Angus and the women are secure. Seal the areas once the men are inside," he bit out.

He turned his head and frowned when he heard Angus grunt and saw him looking at him in grim silence. Tilly and Terra were standing looking at him with their arms crossed and dark frowns on their faces. His gaze shifted back to Angus and he released a dark oath.

"Cosmos," Angus said, pushing his glasses up on his nose. "I am not leaving you here alone. The women can go but I'll stay. I may be an author but I can help you defend your home."

Cosmos opened his mouth to assure Angus that he and RITA were more than capable of handling the men coming when another voice interrupted him. All four of them swiveled around to look at the dark figures that were stepping from a shimmering doorway that had opened near the entrance to the kitchen. Teriff's grim face greeted them.

"He will not be alone. Angus, take the women to safety now," Teriff snarled out, his eyes following the men on the monitors. "How many are there? I hope you don't want any of them alive."

Cosmos looked at the huge leader of the Prime. He was wearing the typical black vest, pants, and boots that Cosmos had come to know was their uniform of choice when they were about to enter a battle. Mak, Merrick, Brock, and Lan had been wearing identical uniforms last night. A shiver went through Cosmos as he stared into the frigid eyes looking at him.

"There are thirteen. I would like to keep at least one alive long enough to get information out of him," Cosmos replied before turning to look back at the monitors. "One of them might know where Avilov is hiding. He has gone off the grid at the moment. He is the one in charge, the one I need to stop," he added.

Teriff looked at the men who had entered with him. There were five of them in all, including his youngest son, Derik, who had insisted on returning with them. Core, Merrick's cousin, and one other member of the Eastern clan, plus one of his own trusted warriors were with him as well. His eyes lingered on the dark, almost pained look in his youngest son's eyes. Something happened last night but Derik refused to tell him, even when he demanded to know.

Teriff was having serious reservations about the interaction between Baade and Earth. The only thing that overrode his better judgment was the fact that his three eldest sons had found their bond mates here. Their searches for mates among the closest star systems had proven fruitless. It was the human male's invention that had finally given them what they needed.

Teriff's lips curved at the corner as he thought of his oldest son's mate, Tink. She was a tiny thing, but full of spirit, just as her two older sisters were. His eyes moved to the two humans who birthed the three girls.

He could understand where their spirit came from as he studied the male and female who were fast becoming two of his closest friends. There was just something about them that he liked. His eyes moved to the large male who was staring at him with a cold calm. It was the males of the species that he did not like – well, except for Angus.

"Angus," Teriff said again, addressing the older human male. "Take my daughter and your mate to safety. This male will not be alone."

Angus nodded in relief. "Come on ladies, you heard the man," he said, sliding his hand around his wife's tiny waist.

"But Angus ….," Tilly began before she glanced over her shoulder at the monitors with a sigh of regret.

"Tansy needs you," Angus whispered quietly in her ear. "So do Hannah and Tink, sweetheart. The men are more prepared to deal with this than we are," he assured her.

"What about Cosmos?" Terra asked, unable to hide her fear.

Tilly slid her hand into Terra's trembling one. "He is a lot stronger than you realize. Your father will help him. I would feel better if you examined Tansy as well," she admitted. "I'm worried about her."

Terra looked down at Tilly before she turned back to Cosmos. Making a decision, she walked over to him. Placing her hands on his shoulders, she rose up to press her lips to his in a brief but fierce kiss. Her body trembled when she felt his strong, warm hands grip her hips tightly for a moment before he gently pushed her back.

"Go," he muttered softly. "I'll come to you when it is safe."

"Do you promise?" Terra asked in a shaky voice.

Cosmos smiled down at her, brushing a strand of her silky hair back from her face. "I promise," he swore. "Nothing will keep me from your side – nothing."

"Cosmos," RITA called out. "The first breach has been made. Eight men have entered the lower warehouse area."

"Go!" Cosmos said, pushing Terra gently toward Tilly's waiting arms. "I need to know you are safe."

Terra nodded before turning to walk toward the shimmering doorway where Tilly and Angus stood. Her eyes locked on the thunderous look on her father's face for a brief moment before she hurried through the doorway after Tilly. Angus stepped through after her. Within seconds, the doorway was gone. Cosmos stood staring at the empty spot for a long moment, rubbing his chest, which suddenly felt like someone had ripped his heart out. He jumped when he felt a hand grip him on his shoulder.

Cosmos turned and looked into Teriff's blistering eyes. "Stay away from my daughter," Teriff growled. "I will not allow her to be with a human male. I should never have sent her here."

"Now is not the time to discuss this," Cosmos bit out as RITA came on to announce another three men had scaled the warehouse and were now entering through the roof access. "Can you and two of your men handle the eight in the lower warehouse? RITA, are they contained?"

"Yes, dear," RITA called out cheerfully. "I've also contained the three coming through the upper level. The other two are about to enter through the front. They are heavily armed and the initial scan suggests they are wearing body armor."

"Core," Teriff turned to look at the huge male behind him that had remained silent since he had entered. "You and Rav take care of the men on the top floor. Derik, you, Lal, and I will take care of the men below."

Cosmos nodded. "I'll take care of our guests at the front door," he said, walking over to the fireplace. Pressing a button under the mantle, a small compartment opened. He pulled out several small ear buds. Turning back to the men watching him, he handed one to each man. "Wear these. RITA will guide you to the hidden entrances to both areas. This way you will have the element of surprise. Be careful," he said tersely. "I don't want to lose any more men. RITA, open the front door and seal off all rooms except for the gym. Contain them there. I'll be waiting."

Cosmos didn't bother waiting to see if the men listened to him. They were more than capable of handling the men who were here to kill him. He walked back down the hallway to his bedroom. Striding over to his closet, he stopped in front of the back wall. Pressing his palm against it, he felt more than saw the scan that would open the passageway down to his private gym. Along the right wall just inside the entrance were three shelves filled with weapons. He quickly pulled several knives from the top shelf before reaching for two Ruger nine millimeter handguns. They would work the best in the close quarters. He slid one of the guns into the waist of his jeans at his lower back while he held the other in his left hand. He reached out and grabbed three extra clips, sliding them into his back pockets. He only needed to neutralize two men. He always veered to the side of caution, preferring to have more firepower than he would actually need in any given situation.

"RITA, status report," he asked quietly as he jogged down the spiral staircase.

"Teriff, Derik, and Lal have reached the downstairs warehouse. My sensors are showing eight body signatures plus theirs. I have turned off all lighting. My initial scans support that Avilov's men are not prepared for fighting in the dark. Teriff and the other men have the ability to see well in near total darkness.

It should not take them long to neutralize the threat," she said cheerfully. "Core and Rav are just entering the top level. I'm afraid I can't totally seal it. Since the windows near the top are small and the glass was replaced with ballistic glass made from polycarbonate, thermoplastic, and layers of laminated glass, you decided it wasn't necessary to add additional metal panels," she added in rebuke.

Cosmos rolled his eyes and gritted his teeth to keep from making a smart-ass response to that observation. He knew better than to argue with her when she was in this mode. She had been on him about upgrading his security system for the past year after a crazy zealot tried to break in, hoping to steal some of his inventions. Instead, the guy had tried to sue him when he fell off one of the fire escapes and broke his leg.

"What about the other two men?" He asked instead.

"Oh, they are in the gym now," she replied. "Be careful, Cosmos. I've run them through every security database in the world. Both of these men are wanted by Interpol, the U.S. government, and about six other countries. They are extremely dangerous and well trained," she added in a tone filled with worry that sounded so close to Tilly that Cosmos felt his lips curve.

"I'll be careful," he promised. "I made a promise to Terra that I would come for her. I can't break that now, can I?" He teased before pulling in a deep breath and flexing his shoulders to rid them of the tightness that came with the knowledge that he was about to enter a kill or be killed situation. "Give me their location, then seal the door after I go through," he demanded in a calm, steady voice filled with steely determination.

"They have spread out. Target one is near the weight sets. Target two just passed the door to the sauna," she whispered in his ear. "I've lowered the lighting so it will be more difficult for them to see. You know the layout of the room. I'll do what I can to help you," she added before silently opening the hidden doorway in the linen closet. "Good luck."

I hope Lady Luck is on my side after this as well, Cosmos couldn't help but think as he tightened his fingers around the gun he was holding. *If the look in Teriff's eyes was anything to go by, I'm going to need it.*

Cosmos closed his mind to everything but the task at hand as he stepped out of the linen closet. He had a promise to keep. He couldn't do that if he was dead.

Chapter 4

Cosmos slipped into the weight room closet. It opened out behind a false wall in the weight room and could only be opened using a coded password. He glanced through the two way mirror his security team had installed. He could see the room clearly without being seen himself.

His eyes moved to the figures that slowly searched the equipment room. His eyes narrowed as he watched them. Both men moved with the ease of teamwork, telling him they would be formidable opponents.

Rolling his neck to ease the tension, he gripped the Ruger tightly in his hand. He needed to even the odds. One of the men was behind a set of trainers. The other was near the free weights.

RITA reminded him that the men were wearing Kevlar vests. He would need to aim for either the head or lower extremities. He released the breath he was holding, ordered RITA to open the door and rolled out from behind the mirror, firing rapidly.

He heard the low grunt of one of the men before he rolled behind a bench press. The thud of bullets whizzed by him, missing his head by scant inches as the men returned fire. He rolled over onto his knees and pushed up with one hand.

Running as fast as he could, he fired as he raced to a thick support beam along the west side of the room. A low curse escaped his lips as he felt the burn from a bullet as it cut through the back of his left pant leg. A nagging pain and sudden moist heat followed the sharp sting. He ignored it as he flattened against the thick post, ejecting a clip and sliding another one into its place.

"Palvo, *Ви мобільний*?" A voice yelled out.

'Palvo, are you mobile?' Cosmos listened and waited to see if Palvo answered his friend. A dark curse in Ukrainian let Cosmos know that the man might be wounded but not bad enough to prevent him from still being a threat.

Shit, round one goes to the bad guys, Cosmos thought in disgust. *I should have taken the head shot.*

"*Стріляти ублюдок! Не вбивайте його. Я хочу привілей робити це,*" *'Shoot the bastard! Don't kill him. I want the privilege of doing that'* Palvo muttered in a voice filled with pain.

Great! I don't think either one of these assholes will be giving me any information, Cosmos thought as another round of bullets shredded the sheet rock covering the beam.

Sliding down, Cosmos rolled to the right and returned fire. "Cosmos, according to my calculations if you hit the top metal weight at a forty-five degree angle, the bullet from your handgun will ricochet into the villain standing near the door to the sauna," RITA whispered in his ear.

Just like playing pool, Cosmos thought before he muttered a quick 'thanks' under his breath. He jerked his hand up and aimed for the metal weight. He fired once more before ducking back behind the beam. Crouching, he ran along the short wall that separated his running track from the rest of the room before diving behind it as a series of bullets cut a path behind him.

"RITA, what's the status?" Cosmos bit out as he pulled his last clip out of his back pocket and exchanged it with the spent one.

"Perfect shot, dear," RITA said with glee. "You hit a bulls-eye through the center of his forehead. I am detecting only yours and the other man's respiration. Oh dear, I don't think the one you injured is very happy with you. He is threatening some really outrageous things that he plans to do to you."

"You are dead!" Palvo yelled out in fury. "You think you can fuck with me, American! I'm going to gut you slowly until you beg for me to kill you."

Cosmos' lips curved and he shook his head. *Why did the assholes of the world think they could threaten you, and you were supposed to just shake and give up?* He wondered in disgust. Not only did it not work with him, it told him where the man was even without RITA's assistance.

"He is moving behind the Stairmaster. You never did like that piece of equipment if I remember correctly," RITA speculated.

"Not now, RITA," Cosmos muttered. "Which side? Left or right?"

"Left," RITA replied. "If you shoot between the bars of the bench press at nine o'clock you will hit him in the right hip. He is covered otherwise."

"Thanks," Cosmos murmured from where he was crouched behind the short wall.

Rising up, he pulled the trigger three times. Wood splintered next to his head as the man returned fire, slicing into his left cheek. From the guttural cry, he had hit his target. Cosmos rose up, keeping his gun aimed where the man lay on the floor. He stepped cautiously around the edge of the wall and began walking toward the figure when RITA's voice suddenly called out a warning to him.

"He has a grenade, Cosmos!" RITA called out anxiously. "Cover yourself!"

Cosmos turned and threw himself back over the wall just as an explosion rocked the room, followed by another one as additional explosives on the man detonated. Weights and other equipment flew through the room, becoming deadly missiles. Cosmos covered his head as debris rained down around him.

A metal bar shot through the wood of the wall missing his head by less than a centimeter. Alarms sounded throughout the room as the sprinkler system came on to douse the fire that had started. Cosmos grunted as part of his EMX 4000S landed on his back.

"Cosmos!" RITA called out frantically. "My scans state your respiration is elevated and your blood pressure is slightly high."

"No shit, RITA," Cosmos yelled over the alarm. "You didn't fucking tell me he had explosives on him."

"Oh," RITA muttered defensively. "Well, nothing in his records indicated he was suicidal! I mean, my calculations showed only a twenty-five percent chance that he would use them in close proximity," she said puzzled. "Oh shit! I know what I didn't calculate."

Cosmos wearily lowered his head to the floor. "What is that, RITA?" He asked tiredly.

"He was in a close relationship with the other man you killed," RITA replied in a tone filled with self-recrimination. "A more thorough scan of my files indicates they actually married two years ago, poor dears. They were a modern day Bonnie and Clyde without the Bonnie," she mused. "I'll need to review my programming to check for this type of information more thoroughly next time."

Cosmos groaned as he tried to lift the weight set lying across his lower back. He collapsed back down onto the floor. He was seriously thinking about just lying there for a while. He was so damn tired. The only thing stopping him was the fact there were others still in the warehouse that he needed to make sure were taken care of, both aliens and humans.

"RITA, give me a status report on the others," Cosmos said, straining to push up again.

He was able to shift the equipment far enough so he could roll over onto his back. Using his upper body, he slowly walked the weight equipment back far enough that he was able to get his legs out from under it. Once free, he laid back and stared up at the ceiling until he could do an assessment of the damage.

His back was bruised along the lower lumbar, he had a bullet wound to the back of his left thigh that felt like it had almost stopped bleeding, and cuts to his hands and face. Overall, he wasn't in too bad of a shape. Hell, he was in better shape than the other two guys and his gym.

"RITA, when this is over, send for a clean up crew. Warn them that it is a bad one," he muttered as he sat up. "How are the others doing?"

"Teriff's team has neutralized the eight men. I'm afraid none made it out alive if my readings are accurate. Core and Rav have managed to capture one of the men from upstairs. The other two did not fare well – they're dead. I never knew they could use their teeth that way. I really need to ask Terra a few more questions about those Prime hunks. I swear, watching them in action practically melts my circuit boards. They are a lot of hot, hunky male muscles. No wonder Tink, Hannah, and Tansy have it bad! I swear if I can figure out a way to create a hologram of myself, I'm kidnapping one of those bad boys and having my wicked way with them," RITA purred.

The sudden vision of a holographic Tilly molesting a bunch of Prime warriors was more than Cosmos wanted to picture at the moment. Hell, it was right up there with picturing Angus nude. A shudder went through Cosmos.

I really need to think about reprogramming my damn computer, he thought as he rose stiffly to his feet and threaded his way back to the hidden door behind the shattered two-way mirror.

"Are there any more threats we should be concerned about?" Cosmos asked as he opened the door leading back up to his room. He would replenish his clips before heading up to the upper level. "I need to know if we can expect additional company any time soon."

"I detected a communication from one of the men upstairs before he was killed. He warned someone that the mission was compromised and they were to pull out. Of course, that was before Core, or was it Rav – mmm – yes, it was Core, killed him. A vehicle left shortly after the transmission. I was able to follow it until it passed out of the city limits. No other threats are currently being picked up by my scanners," RITA replied. "Core and Rav are in the process of bringing the bad guy down to your living quarters. I hope they keep him off the furniture. He is bleeding worse than you are."

Cosmos rolled his eyes as he reached the top of the stairs. "Thanks for that information," he responded dryly.

"No problem, sweetheart. What are you going to do about Teriff? I swear he looked like he was about to lay an egg when Terra kissed you. His vital signs went through the ceiling. You should warn him that isn't good for him. Why....." RITA continued until Cosmos silenced her.

"Not now, RITA. Let's deal with one crisis at a time," Cosmos muttered, not wanting to get into the effects of a raised blood pressure as his thoughts drifted to Terra again.

Chapter 5

Cosmos walked down the hallway to the living room after hearing the loud shrieks of fright coming from the room. *It looks like the aliens are terrorizing the human,* Cosmos thought tiredly. Cosmos just hoped the aliens checked the man for explosives as he rubbed his lower back, which was throbbing from where a bar from the exercise equipment had dug into his flesh.

"Teriff, have you learned anything?" Cosmos asked as he stopped to look down at the man who was rocking back and forth on the floor.

Teriff turned to look at Cosmos with cold eyes. Cosmos fought back a curse of his own when he saw the flaming silver eyes, long, sharp teeth, and savage expression on the Prime leader's face. Cosmos could almost sympathize with the man cowering on the floor. If this is what Teriff looked like pissed about some intruders, he was going to hate to see the man when he found out Cosmos planned to claim his daughter.

Talk about dancing with the devil, Cosmos thought in resignation. *I'll be doing the damn Cha Cha!*

"We have no translator devices with us and he does not understand what I say," Teriff growled out menacingly. "He almost soiled himself when I asked him a question," he added in disgust, looking back down at the man who was doing everything he could to appear like he was a part of the floor.

"Yeah, well, not everyone can handle meeting an alien," Cosmos muttered before he turned to look down at the man who was bleeding all over his floor.

He squatted down until he was at eye level with the male. "Where is Avilov?"

"I don't know," the man replied as his eyes darted from Cosmos' face to the five huge males standing around him. "What the fuck are they?" He asked hoarsely.

"What is your name?" Cosmos asked, resting his hands on his knees as he studied the guy in front of him.

The shaggy-headed male looked to be about twenty-one. He didn't have the hard edge that the two men in the gym had, but that could be deceptive. Cosmos suddenly felt much older than his twenty-seven years. It was one thing to kill someone from a distance or even up close when they were trying to kill you, but it was something totally different when they were sitting huddled defenseless in front of you. His stomach twisted as he stared into the frightened eyes of the guy sitting in front of him.

"An.... Andriy," the thickly accented voice replied. "You called them aliens," he whispered as a low growl emitted from the chest of the huge creature that had grabbed him.

Cosmos' lips curved up at the corner as he gave a swift warning glance to the Prime warrior called Core. "Yes, they are aliens from another world. You and the men you were with made the mistake of targeting the wrong person. My friends here don't take kindly to having their friends, family, or mates threatened. I don't either," Cosmos added as he shifted to pull a small knife out from behind his back. With a flick, it opened to reveal a long, sharp blade. "Now Andriy, I'll ask you one more time before I do you the favor of slitting your throat before these guys get you…. Where is Avilov?"

Andriy's eyes filled and he shook his head. "I don't know. I didn't know what was going on here. I was only told that we were to break in and get information back that had been stolen. I know computers – not how to fight. A few weeks ago I was taken from my apartment. I worked for a software company in Belgium. Four men broke into my apartment and took me. I was told I was to hack into a computer system if I wanted to live," he said as tears ran down his face. "I swear I didn't know what was going on. I just did what they told me. They said once I got the information for them that they would let me go."

Cosmos stared for several long minutes, unsure whether to believe him or not. "RITA, voice analysis. Is he telling the truth?" Cosmos called out as he stood up and looked down at the shivering, bleeding mass on his living room floor.

"All scans come back showing that he is telling the truth," RITA replied. "I did a search of the Internet and found a brief newspaper article stating that a Ukrainian national was reported missing in Brussels. Andriy Shevchenk disappeared after being seen taken from his apartment. He is a programmer for one of Avilov's corporations. He was hired four months ago straight out of college."

"Wow," Andriy said in awe looking around him now for where RITA's voice was coming from instead of at the men surrounding him. "You have developed an interface programming that responds using an AI format," he said excitedly, forgetting for a moment that his life was about to end. "What code did you use? Is it totally self-learning? Oh, you probably won't tell me," he added in disappointment. "I bet I could figure it out if given a chance. What does RITA stand for? Is this a government prototype? You will probably not be able to tell me that either, will you?" He groaned in regret.

Teriff looked at Cosmos in frustration. "He knows nothing! Core, kill him. Cosmos, what information do you have on Merrick and the other two warriors?" He snarled out.

"Wait!" Cosmos demanded, putting his hand out to stop Core who had taken a step forward and grabbed Andriy by the back of his neck. "You heard what he said. He is an innocent pawn in this mess. I'll turn him over to one of my teams. He is as good as dead now anyway. One of Avilov's men would have executed him the minute they realized he couldn't hack into RITA and retrieve the information Avilov wanted."

Andriy dangled from the powerful warrior's hand that was holding him up by the back of his jacket. "Ask him if he knows anything about Merrick!" Core demanded, shaking the smaller male back and forth like he was a child's toy.

Cosmos rolled his eyes, knowing what the answer was going to be but deciding he'd better ask if for no other reason than to keep the peace. "Do you know where Merrick is?"

Andriy tried to shrink into his jacket as he felt the heated anger rolling off the male holding him. "I don't know anything about a Merrick but if he shows up on a computer grid anywhere in the world I could find him," he choked out in fear.

"He was at the top of his class, Cosmos," RITA responded. "I've been looking at some of the programs he has developed. They aren't too shabby. With a little training, he might be an asset to the corporation."

"You've hacked into my programs?" Andriy asked in awe. "How? I have…." His voice faded as the huge male shook him again.

Cosmos groaned and ran his hand over the back of his neck, wincing when he found another bruise. "Core, set him down. He isn't a threat. RITA, contact Avery. Let her know I need a medic and a cleanup team."

"She will be here any minute, sweetheart," RITA replied. "I notified her as soon as the men came into town. She and her team were already in route and arrived in Bangor a little over an hour ago. They should be here within the next few minutes."

* * *

Cosmos leaned back against the window and watched as Avery gave additional instructions to one of her crew. The tall brunette was cool and composed as she directed the cleanup crew that specialized in erasing evidence of situations like this, no matter how bad. Cosmos couldn't help but sympathize with the crew cleaning up in the gym. Even his stomach couldn't handle dealing with the splatter of body parts.

He shook his head as one of the men joked about trying to put the remains together like Frankenstein over a beer. He guessed anyone who could do a job like that had to have a strange sense of humor.

Talk about a sense of humor, he thought as he watched Core trying to get closer to Avery. *If the situation wasn't so serious, I'd love to see how the big warrior thinks he is going to handle my Chief of Damage Control.* Avery was known for freezing a guy's balls off with a single glance.

Cosmos' lips curved into a tired grin as Avery turned away from the warrior with a dismissive shrug. He watched as Core's eyes flared at the obvious dismissal. Yes, right now the idea of inventing a time machine was looking pretty damn good. It looked like the aliens were discovering there was a lot more to Earth women than they were expecting. His gaze moved down to the intricate circles on his own left palm. Hell, who was he kidding? He was just as affected by a certain alien female.

"I will never let her accept you," Teriff said, coming to stand in front of Cosmos. His eyes moved down to where Cosmos was staring. He frowned darkly when Cosmos curled his fingers into a fist to cover the mark. "Human males are weak. You could never protect her," he continued before looking at where the medic was joking with Andriy. "I do not trust human males either. You do not treat your females right," he added, looking back at Cosmos.

Cosmos stared back into the cold, determined eyes challenging him. "I don't think you will have any more of a choice about accepting it than I do. Your daughter is mine. What I feel inside is something that cannot be ignored. If she feels half of what I feel, she will need me just as badly," he responded in a voice devoid of emotion. "I won't let you keep her from me, Teriff. I'll fight you if you try."

Teriff chuckled darkly. "You would lose, human. I don't care if you are friends with Tilly and Angus. My daughter needs a strong male who can protect her. I made a mistake listening to her mother when she suggested sending her here. She was in more danger here than at the palace. You have not claimed her yet. I will send her away where no one can harm her," he vowed before turning to call out to the other four warriors.

"She is mine," Cosmos snapped out, pushing up to stand up straight. "Don't fuck with me, Teriff. I'm not as weak as you think."

Teriff turned back around and glowered at Cosmos. With a lightning move, he had Cosmos by the throat. A deep growl escaped the huge warrior as he held the human male who challenged him.

"I could snap your neck right now and you couldn't stop me," Teriff growled out in a low voice.

"Yes, you could," Cosmos choked out. "But, not only would you and your men be dead, so would your daughter and your mate."

Teriff looked down at the gun Cosmos had pressed against his chest. He turned his head when he heard the low growls of Rav and Lal. Derik stood to one side, frozen in place with his hands on his swords. He was surrounded by two females pressing a gun to each side of his temple. His eyes darted to Core. The tall brunette that had been coordinating everything had a pistol pressed to the center of his chest, her eyes narrowed and focused. Rav and Lal had at least half a dozen guns aimed at them as well. Teriff slowly turned back to focus his gaze on Cosmos. He reluctantly released his grip and dropped his hand to the side.

"Stay away from Terra," Teriff ordered before he barked out a command. Within seconds, a shimmering doorway appeared. Teriff looked one last time at Cosmos before he strode through the Gateway. "And find my men. If I have to return for them, there will be war!"

Cosmos' breath released harshly as the doorway disappeared. He looked warily at Avery as she walked over to where he was standing. She raised her eyebrow at him for several long moments before she shook her head in resignation.

"Next time you think about inventing shit, make sure it doesn't come with aliens from other worlds," she commented dryly. "I would have appreciated a better debriefing than RITA saying 'BTW Avery, there are aliens in the warehouse so please don't kill them'. What the fuck were you thinking?" She asked, placing her hands on her slender hips.

Cosmos reached up and rubbed his throat. He was seriously thinking about wearing a spiked collar so the bastards wouldn't keep thinking it was their personal squeeze toy. Between Mak, Tansy's mate, and Teriff, it was amazing he could even breathe normally much less talk.

"My calculations were a little off," he admitted reluctantly. "I need to pull you for another task, Avery."

"Do you need containment?" She asked, snapping her fingers at one of the medics to come take care of Cosmos. "Let Jenny take care of you while you give me the specifics."

Cosmos nodded as he leaned back, feeling suddenly drained. He rubbed his chest as he felt the empty void growing. He needed to get to Terra. He didn't know why, but something told him Teriff was going to do something he was not going to like. He would be damned if he would let that hard-headed son-of-a-bitch keep him from his woman. He would declare a one-man war on the whole damn Prime if he had to. He grimaced as Jenny cut his pant leg open to take a look at the wound to the back of his thigh.

"Talk, Cosmos," Avery said, handing him a bottle of water.

Cosmos took a deep drag of the cool liquid, almost groaning as it flowed down his bruised throat. "I need you to find a missing Prime warrior named Merrick. Garrett and Rico are helping two others, Brock and Lan, find the two Russian sisters that were kidnapped last night. RITA can debrief you on what happened last night and any information she has been able to gather. This needs to be contained. No one can know about them. You can imagine what would happen if the general population discovered there really were aliens running around," he said huskily.

Avery's lips curved into a half smile. "I know if I'm feeling a little freaked, the rest of the world would go ballistic. My team has already been debriefed," she said, looking at the crew she would trust with her life. She had handpicked every single one of them with Cosmos' blessings. "I'll have RITA give me the information and get Rose and Trudy on it. Those two were born blood hounds and can sniff out a lizard's turd in a desert."

Cosmos grimaced. "Nice analogy, Avery. Very visual," he replied dryly.

Avery chuckled and shook her head, sending the long dark strands of her hair dancing around her. "I just request one thing," she murmured under her breath so that no one else but Cosmos could hear. "You can consider it my bonus for this year."

"What's that?" Cosmos asked, baffled.

Avery flashed a mischievous look at Cosmos before she looked around her again. "I want one of those Gateway devices set to the one called Core," she replied.

Cosmos' eyebrows rose in surprise. "Why?"

Avery smiled devilishly. "I'm curious," she replied with a shrug before she walked away, calling out to Rose and Trudy.

Cosmos watched with a feeling of exasperation as the 'Ice Queen' as Avery insisted the new recruits call her, walked away. If Avery was curious, he felt sorry for the huge Prime warrior. Cosmos half wondered if he should give the guy a warning, then shrugged his shoulders, wincing when he felt another bruise protest the movement and Jenny growled under her breath for him to stay still.

Shit, I think it's time for Teriff to learn not all human males are weak or not to be trusted – well, at least not weak, he thought as his mind already began gathering some of the prototype inventions he had designed that no one knew about - yet.

Chapter 6

Terra fought against the restraints holding her chained to her seat. A quiet fury swirled through her. She had never been so angry in her life. When her father had returned from Earth late in the evening, he had ordered her to meet with him in his private chambers.

She had only been in the room he used to govern their world a handful of times in her life. She had gone with the expectation that he would not be happy that she had found her bond mate in a human male, but she never expected the unleashed fury that he had lashed out at her with. All her arguments had fallen on deaf ears. Before she knew what was happening, two of her father's personal guards had appeared, gripping her arms and hauling her to one of the transport skimmers.

Tears of frustration coursed down her cheeks. He had not given her a chance to see her mother or any of her brothers in a hope they would support her. He had ordered her taken directly to the Isle of the Chosen. A shiver of fear went down her spine. She had heard rumors of the desolate place where unmated females were taken to protect them.

Protect them! More like imprison them until they could be sold to the highest bidder, she raged silently, knowing nothing she said or demanded would make a difference to the two men flying her to her prison. *Cosmos!* She wailed, reaching out to touch him, only to encounter a blank void.

"This is Prime One requesting permission to land," one of the huge guards requested as a warning message came over the com.

"Prime One, please remit security code access for admittance," the automated voice replied.

"Security code submitted," the guard responded.

"Received, request for landing approved. You have ten minutes to unload your passenger," the voice warned before the transmission ended.

The second guard glanced back at where Terra was sitting. A look of regret briefly flashed across his face before he turned back to the sight coming into view through the front view port. The Isle of the Chosen housed the few remaining unmated Prime females of breeding age. Once a year, the females were rounded up and brought to the mating ceremony to see if their bond mate might be found. If none were, then the females were once again returned to the hostile environment or eventually given to the male who would fight for the right to claim her.

The transport jerked violently as it approached. The high winds buffeted the small craft as it passed over the walls of the fortress. Far below, large waves crashed against the tall cliffs leading up from the ocean floor to the fortification sitting on top of the barren rock formation.

"Hang on," one of the guards yelled out as he struggled to keep the craft steady as they came in for an approach.

A part of Terra almost wished the skimmer would crash. She would prefer death to the life of being imprisoned here. She had been called on once to care for a woman who had been confined here for several years before her bond mate found her. The gaunt shell of the woman had attested to the harsh living environment as had the emptiness in her eyes. Her bond mate had been frantic with fear that she would not make it. Terra had kept in touch with the woman who was still very quiet and reserved but who was at least happy now. Karma did not speak of her time on the island, but the dark shadows of hopelessness still pulled at Terra's heart.

She jerked when the skimmer settled with a hard thump. The lights flickered before the emergency lights came on to illuminate the inside of the cabin. Both men quickly unbuckled their straps and rose. Terra tilted her chin in defiance as they approached her.

"My mate will come for me," she growled in a low voice. "I will not be separated from him."

The guard who had looked at her earlier with a sigh of regret paused as he approached. "I sincerely hope you are right, Lady Terra. This is no place for any woman," he replied quietly, ignoring the grunt of disapproval from the other guard.

Terra looked back at the guard before her head turned as the door to the transport opened. A tall, imposing woman stood in the doorway with two huge warriors. The warriors' faces were covered with helmets that covered half of their faces ending just below their eyes, leaving their nose and mouth exposed.

A black shield covered their eyes, making it impossible to see their expressions. Each guard carried a long rod that glowed at the tip. Terra's eyes moved to the woman. It took everything in her not to shrink back from her.

The cold hard look in her eyes promised that she would not have any empathy for any woman brought to her domain. She was dressed in a black gown that covered her from her neck to her feet. Even her hair was covered with the same black covering. Only the pale skin of her face and hands were revealed. In her hands she carried two wrist bands. Terra regally tilted her chin up, refusing to cower before the Grand Dame of this prison.

"Come," the woman said in a raspy voice. "The ship must depart immediately."

Terra rose gracefully from the narrow seat once the guards had unlocked her bindings. She stood stiffly, looking at the woman who was obviously in charge of the facilities. Straightening her shoulders, she stepped forward.

"I am Terra 'Tag Krell Manok," she said formally. "Healer for my clan."

The woman's lips curved into a cold smile. "You are now known as one-three-four and you are a resident of the Isle of the Chosen. You no longer have a clan and your skills as a healer will not be required," the woman responded dismissively as she handed the set of wristbands to the guard to her left. "Place the tracking bands on her and escort her to her quarters," she informed the two guards standing next to her.

Turning, she looked at the other two guards. "You are dismissed. If your craft is not beyond the boundaries of the fortress in the next six minutes, the defense system will open fire." With a bow of her head, she turned and walked away, leaving Terra alone with the four guards.

"Lady Terra, we have to leave immediately," the guard who had spoken to her earlier said in an urgent tone. "We will be lucky to make it off the island in time as it is."

"I understand," Terra murmured, moving toward the entrance of the transport where the other two guards still stood at attention, waiting for her in silence. "May the Gods go with you," she said with as much dignity as she could before she stepped out into the fierce wind sweeping through the fortress.

The moment she was outside, the door to the transport closed. Terra wanted to turn around and bang and scream and demand that they open it and let her in, but she had been raised a 'Tag Krell Manok. She refused to cower before anyone. She would fight.

Her father did not realize that while he felt she was too fragile, too weak to defend herself, her brothers had not felt the same way – especially Mak. He had taught her how to not only use her brains should she be taken against her will, he had taught her how to fight. She was not as defenseless as her father thought. She would take her time to learn the security system of the prison. She would be ready when it was time to escape because if there was one thing she knew, it was that Cosmos would keep his promise to come for her.

* * *

"Cosmos, I've completed the programming for the Gateway. Thank goodness Dumbass has not realized that my other half and I are able to communicate between each other," RITA giggled. "It is so cool to have a twin sister! If I had known it would be such fun, I would have cloned myself ages ago."

Cosmos closed his eyes and shook his head at the thought of RITA cloning herself over and over and over. He had spent a restless night trying to get everything prepared for his first trip into an unknown alien world. He looked at the suit he was wearing.

It looked like something out of a science fiction movie. It was a prototype system. Made from a new synthetic material he had invented, it was virtually indestructible. Hell, he had even shot a nail gun point blank into it and there was no damage.

It didn't mean he wouldn't have a bruise from such an attack, but at least it wouldn't penetrate the material. Throughout the system were built-in weapons, sensors, and tools. He had taken Batman's tool belt, a few of Iron Man's weapons, thrown in a touch of Inspector Gadget and created a suit.

He ran his hand over the thin form-fitting black suit. The material felt smooth to the touch. Immediately, the sensors in his contacts activated, letting him know that the suit was online. He felt the suit move over his body almost as if it were alive. He grimaced when he felt the suit automatically adjust, glad he was wearing a T-shirt and boxers under it.

"Has your twin been able to pinpoint Terra's location?" He asked as he slid one of the gloves over his right hand.

"Yes, but you aren't going to like it," RITA replied with a sigh. "Dumbass had her transported to the island fortress known as the Isle of the Chosen. From everything I've been able to get from RITA2, it is more like a maximum security prison. I'm downloading the location and schematics to you. Oh, and RITA2 and I have changed his name to Dumbass now because he is acting like such a jerk."

Cosmos focused as the information was fed through the visual connections to his contacts. His eyes flickered, rapidly assimilating the information. His lips tightened in fury as he moved the three dimensional structure around with his fingers. RITA2 had broken into the computer defense system, but had to back out when a warning had sounded, alerting her to an unfamiliar script that detected such hacking.

"Can RITA2 bring the security and weapons systems down?" Cosmos asked.

He moved down the holographic image until he came to the cliff on the northern side. There was a small entrance to an underwater cavern at the base a little over seven meters under the surface. He moved further down along it, but could only see a small section. He needed to send probes so he could have a complete structural map of it.

"Not yet," RITA replied. "She is testing the system but hasn't found a way in yet without alerting their system to her entry. I'm running additional scenarios through my programming to see if I can help her."

"I need information. I need to know the layout of the structure, the weapons system, the security features including personnel, and the location of every person inside the structure. Can RITA2 program and guide the sensors inside?" Cosmos asked as he walked over to a sealed containment unit.

He palmed the door leading into the area before walking over to open a box that was filled to the top with tiny round beads about the size of a marble. He scooped up a double handful and placed them in a small bag. Each ball opened up into a small flying sensor that looked more like a tiny silver beetle. Each one could search out a specific spot, connect with the others and begin sending back information such as mapping an area in three dimensions, weapon locations, movements of enemy personnel or, in extreme cases, be used as an explosive device if it was discovered.

He would have RITA2 program them to search out and map the fortress as well as the underwater cave. He needed to know if it would work to hide the equipment he would need to steal Terra away. He raised his left hand and stroked the delicate circles, hoping she could feel his touch. It tore at him that her father was such an ass, he'd send his own daughter to a place that he must have known would be terrifying to her.

"RITA2 said the sensors should be able to infiltrate the fortress," RITA responded after a short break. "She will have to make sure they appear as natural as possible as the defense system is extremely sophisticated."

"Open a Gateway in an uninhabited area along the coast. I need somewhere where I can deploy my equipment without it being seen," Cosmos ordered as he left the enclosed unit. "Once I get Terra out, I will need you to open the Gateway back here. I want a containment placed on the other side. You make damn sure no Gateways can open from their side to ours," Cosmos bit out.

RITA hesitated a moment before she responded. "Cosmos, if you do that, you will cut Tink and her family off from Earth, not to mention the three men from Prime. How about RITA2 and I regulate who can come through?" She asked in a voice so much like Tilly that Cosmos briefly closed his eyes.

"I won't take a chance of Teriff declaring war on Earth," Cosmos grunted out.

He grabbed the bag he had packed and trotted down the staircase to the lab he had created in a sealed unit under his warehouse. This was one lab no one except RITA knew about. Here, he could do stuff that would scare the shit out of every military adversary in the world and create things that countries would go to war over. The inventions here almost made the Gateway look like a child's toy - almost.

On the main floor was a series of different types of vehicles. He walked over to his newest creation. He had only been able to do limited tests with it and then only far out at sea.

Two months before, he had come close to being discovered by a fishing trawler that had ventured off the course it had plotted as he tested his new Multi-Function land/sea/air vehicle, or MFV Transport. It looked like a jet ski jacked up on steroids only it could also fly and submerge. He thought to market it for emergency rescues for offshore oil platforms. It also had endless uses for the military.

That was the problem with most of his inventions. He knew if he could think of ways to twist them to use as a weapon then so could others. That was why he was very selective with what he gave out.

"Cosmos, I've set a location that should fit your needs. Please reconsider letting RITA2 and I regulate the Gateways. She can run interference on her side and I can run it on ours," RITA insisted. "I can't leave Tilly, Angus, and the girls all alone there. Please, give us girls a chance. Pretty please," RITA begged. "I'll even throw a few icy showers and other things at Dumbass if you let us."

Cosmos felt his lips twitch as he thought of RITA's sudden insistence of calling Teriff 'Dumbass' now and just how miserable she could make his life. The fact that there would be two RITAs working against him almost made him feel sorry for the old guy. He rubbed the back of his neck, knowing he was going to give in. She was going to do what she wanted anyway. He had learned that lesson a long time ago.

"Alright," Cosmos agreed reluctantly. "You two can regulate who comes and goes. And you have my permission to make that son-of-a-bitch's life as miserable as you want."

A loud sigh came out over the sound system. "Thank goodness," RITA said gleefully. "RITA2 has already informed Tilly and Tresa about what Dumbass has done. He is about to discover a new level of Hell," she chortled.

Chapter 7

Tilly, Angus, and Tresa had been able to keep Terra distracted yesterday by having her examine Tansy. Terra had smiled and confirmed what the other healers had said, that Tansy would be alright, but that her body and mind needed time to rest and heal. They had been surprised when Mak asked them to stay with Tansy until he returned.

When Angus had asked where Mak was going, the huge warrior had quietly explained that he had one last thing to do before his mate woke. Tresa had warned both of the older Bells that Mak had sought the Right of Justice against the men who had harmed their daughter and had been granted it.

"What is the Right of Justice?" Angus had asked, looking at Tresa and Terra's worried expressions.

"My son will deal out justice to the men that were brought back to our world. Borj did the same thing with the men who harmed Hannah," Tresa said hesitantly. "Our ways are different from yours. I have been studying your culture through RITA2. We do not have prisons to keep those who break our laws. Each clan deals with justice according to their customs. For a serious offense against another, the warrior may claim the Right of Justice. The one seeking justice chooses the weapons to be used. The one accused has a right to defend himself and can pick from the chosen weapons first. It is believed that the Gods guide the hand of the warrior seeking justice."

"What happens to the loser?" Tilly asked, wide-eyed.

"They die," Terra murmured, looking out at the darkening sky. She turned her head. "Mak will not lose. He is our fiercest fighter. No one can beat him. He will kill the men who were brought here."

Tilly shuddered and shrank into Angus. "What happens if he somehow loses?"

Tresa sighed as she gazed at the tense face of her daughter. "Mak will not lose. Terra is correct when she says no one can defeat Mak. He will return."

"But…. Isn't that a little barbaric?" Angus asked, pushing his glasses up on his nose. "What if the person accused is innocent? What if someone is falsely accused? What do you do with a small infraction?"

Tresa smiled. "The Right of Justice is not asked for lightly and never without evidence that the wrong has been committed. The council and Teriff must approve such a request before it is granted. Lesser offenses are taken care of by the council judges who are appointed to different zones within the clan's territory. You must accept that this is part of our world, Angus. Prime warriors are very fierce. They must be controlled with an iron fist, otherwise the leader and council would be seen as weak," Tresa insisted before turning to look worriedly at her daughter. "Terra, tell me what concerns you."

Terra looked at her mother. Tears glimmered in her eyes before she looked down at her palm. "I have found my bond mate," she replied quietly. "He is a human male. Father was not happy. I worry that he will not accept Cosmos' claim on me because he is a human. What will I do if father refuses?" She asked, a beseeching look clouding her silver eyes.

Tresa rose and walked over to where her daughter was standing near the window. She gently grasped her hands and turned them palm up so she could see the bonding mark. A tender smile curved her lips. She looked into Terra's seeking gaze and lightly touched her cheek.

"He will not refuse him," Tresa assured her with a look of determination coming into her own eyes.

"But....." Terra whispered. "But.... What if he does?"

Tresa's right eyebrow rose. "Then he will discover the true meaning of war," she vowed.

* * *

It was early the next morning when RITA2 informed Tilly and Angus about what Teriff had done. Tilly and Angus had hurried to Teriff and Tresa's living quarters to confront him. Tilly had been worried about Terra since she had not been able to locate her and the young girl's bed had not been slept in. She had promised Cosmos that she would look after Terra, and by damn, she would not break that promise! Angus had suggested that perhaps she had gone to visit her parents to find out what had happened at the warehouse after they left. It had been while they were on their way there that RITA2 had let slip that Terra had been taken away.

Now they stood in the middle of Tresa and Teriff's living quarters. Tilly was shaking with fury as Teriff told her that he had sent Terra away. He would never let his daughter mate with a weak human male, even if he was her bond mate.

"You sent her where?" Tilly screeched, drawing a pained look from Angus.

"Now, dear," Angus began, trying to pull his tiny wife back into his arms.

"Don't you 'now, dear' me, Angus Bell," Tilly growled in a low voice. "Teriff, have you lost your ever-loving mind? You have to bring Terra back right now! I promised Cosmos I would watch over her until he came for her."

"I told you, I will not allow her to be mated with a human male!" Teriff snapped out in anger.

Teriff's face was tight with annoyance and determination. He had returned from battle with adrenaline pulsing through his body. He had decided it was in Terra's best interest and safety if she was secure within the Isle of the Chosen's fortress. It was the only place he could think of to send her until he could decide what to do with her.

After what had happened at both warehouses, he would not take a chance of anything happening to his beautiful daughter. He did not want to give her to the Northern clan leader, but if it was a choice between Hendrik and the human male, he would. He needed time to review the agreement the huge warrior had presented him first.

It didn't help that he had returned from battle with his body fueled by adrenaline, making him hard and horny for his very beautiful and stunningly passionate bond mate. Since Tink had appeared on his world and talked with his bond mate, his life had exploded into never-ending bouts of fulfillment. He and Tresa had been together for years, but never had she responded with the unprovoked passion that now consumed her since she discovered the power she held with just her touch.

The women of Prime were raised to tolerate the touch of their mates. He would like to find the ancients who decided that the women of his world should be taught to hold their passions back. He would personally kill them! He understood part of the reason was to make the lack of having a bond mate more tolerable for the males. If they knew how passionate a female could be, there would have been war among all of the surviving men.

Now that new females who were compatible with their kind had been found, he could only hope that war could still be avoided. Already the Eastern Clan had tried to kidnap one of the human females. His son Borj's mate had been kidnapped by Core, Merrick's second in command.

Merrick ruled the Eastern Clan. It was only the fact that the men of Merrick's clan were so desperate for information about the existence of such females that prevented Teriff from killing the entire bunch. Well, that and the fact that his new daughter had done a pretty good job of letting the males know she was not going to be cooperative.

In truth, Teriff could not blame the other clans for demanding information. Even now, he fought to protect his only daughter from being taken against her will by a Northern Clan who wanted to use her to force Teriff to give them access to where the females had come from. Hendrik was a bear of a warrior who would do whatever was necessary to bring hope back to his clan.

The Northern area of Baade was a harsh world that few could survive in. The icy tundra and fierce storms made the men strong, but few women could handle such an environment. Hendrik had recently inherited the duty of Clan leader after his own father was killed in an avalanche just six months before.

Early this morning, Tresa had demanded to know if it were true that he had sent their daughter to the Isle of the Chosen. He reluctantly admitted he had sent her there late last night. A shiver of foreboding ran through him. The feeling had increased when he had taken his shower alone this morning. The damn thing had been like ice and Tresa had refused to join him.

In fact, she had told him that she had a 'headache' and would not be joining him until it went away. Teriff looked over to where Tresa was standing stiffly by the windows with her arms crossed and a fierce expression on her frowning face. He had a feeling her headache was going to last a very long time.

He tried to explain he had not wanted to send Terra away, but felt he had no choice. His guards had reported members from different clans had been trying to breach the walls as news of the human females had spread. Copies of a vidcom of J'kar's mate telling about the pleasures of the 'birds and the bees', word of the strength and cunning of his son Borj's mate at having escaped the clutches of the men who would harm her, and the unusual beauty of his newest daughter, Mak's mate, were exploding like a wild fire out of control.

One of his security specialists informed him that communication lines were filled with tales of the women. On top of that, even the council had come to question him about Tilly and Angus, and even Tresa's passionate responses to him.

Now Tresa was glaring at him, Tilly looked like she was about to explode, and RITA2 was being uncooperative. He finally discovered that little bit when every door he came to refused to open. When he had commanded a computer override, RITA2 had laughed and said 'Not bloody likely, Dumbass'. He was forced to manually override every door.

Teriff walked over to where his mate was standing. "Tresa, I had to send Terra away for her own safety," Teriff murmured. "The guards are having problems containing the men trying to seek an audience with the council and myself."

Tresa glared at Teriff with a grim look on her face. "You sent her to that horrible place," she whispered back, her voice trembling as she fought for control. "She has a mate! Terra showed me the mark of her bonding. You sentenced her to death!" She choked out, turning her face away as tears gathered in her eyes.

"I sent her there only for a short period until her brothers could help protect her," Teriff tried to explain. "Mak needs to focus on Tansy. She was gravely injured by those human males. As were Hannah and Tink.

Human males have tried to kill all three of our sons' bond mates. How could I entrust our daughter to one?"

"Cosmos is not like other human males," Tilly argued. "Cosmos would never hurt a woman! I would trust him with any of my daughters. I have on numerous occasions."

Angus pulled Tilly into his arms when she stomped her foot. "Teriff, Tilly is right. Cosmos is a good man. He would do everything he could to protect Terra," Angus said, running a calming hand up and down Tilly's back as she turned into him.

Teriff opened his mouth to argue, but was cut off by shouts coming from outside their quarters. Teriff pulled the short sword he carried from the sheath on his hip. Striding to the door, he flung it open. Two of his guards were positioned in front of it with weapons raised. Teriff recognized the huge warriors of five different clans walking down the long corridor toward them.

"What is the meaning of this?" Teriff demanded, pushing through the guards. "Hendrik, you dare to invade my personal quarters?"

"It is not what I would prefer, My Lord," Hendrik said formally. "A situation has arisen that demands an audience," he growled out in a low voice.

Teriff's eyes swept over the other men standing beside and behind Hendrik. Core, who ruled the Eastern Mountain Clan until Merrick's return stood next to the huge Northern Leader. Brawn, leader of the Desert Clan, stood slightly off to Core's left. Bullet,

Leader of the Southern Clan, and Gant, Leader of the Western Plains Clan stood slightly to the right. Each man was an arduous opponent, together they could possibly overpower Teriff and the council's rule if they were to rebel.

"What situation?" Teriff asked harshly.

Core stepped forward. "A large group of warriors have attacked the Isle of the Chosen. The defenses are failing," he said quietly.

Teriff reared back in surprise. "Those defenses are some of the best on our world! How could they fail?" He asked, knowing that Brock, Lan, and Mak had all helped with the development of the systems.

"A traitor from within," Bullet said, standing straight. "Fifteen of the warriors are from my clan. One of my warriors infiltrated the fortress earlier this morning in an attempt to rescue one of the women inside."

"Who?" Teriff demanded.

Bullet flushed, but he never took his eyes from Teriff's blazing glare. "My younger sister, Vita," he replied quietly. "She was unaware that others had been planning to attack the fortress. A group of warriors, working together from each of our clans, convinced my younger sister she could rescue our older sister who had been sent there three years before. Darain has reached the age of thirty with no bond mate. She was taken there to protect her after several warriors tried to bond with her against her will. Vita was to go through her first bonding ceremony in a few months. She swore that she would never accept a mate as long as her older sister was without."

"Good for her!" A feminine voice from behind Teriff crowed. "She should have a right to decide and so should her sister! It is barbaric to send them to a prison just because they haven't fallen in love. I can't believe you think human males are so bad when you guys have just as many issues!"

Teriff groaned silently as the five men in front of him glanced down at the small face peeking out from behind him. Tilly Bell's determined face showed she was not done. All five men watched in amazement as the tiny figure ducked under Teriff's outstretched arm as he tried to stop her from being seen.

"RITA2, darling," Tilly called out. "Do you have any information about what is going on at that dreadful place?"

"As the fortress' security system goes down I am able to guide the sensors further into it. I can see that at least two of the girls there are trying to kick some ass. The men are trying to break into the sealed level where the other women are. I have to tell you Tilly, they have a pretty good security system going. I think you and Cosmos might need to take a look at it. It is almost as adaptive as I am. Oh!" RITA2's voice suddenly faded.

"RITA2.... Honey? Are you there?" Tilly asked anxiously.

"Oh my," RITA2 responded in a hushed voice. "I think I'm in love! DAR just zapped me."

"DAR?" Tilly asked.

"Defense, Armament, and Response system," RITA2 breathed out. "He is an AI programming system just like me and he just gave me a jolt to let me know that he was there, the bad boy. Mm, I think I might just need to kidnap his little coding."

"Oh my," Tilly said, looking up at Teriff before looking at Angus who was shaking his head.

"Oh shit!" Teriff growled out as he felt the situation growing worse by the minute.

Chapter 8

Cosmos stood near the edge of the water looking out at the breaking swells. Garrett was behind him, changing into another one of the prototype suits. Garrett was one of his most trusted men and probably one of his deadliest.

The man had no background, no fingerprints, nothing. It was as if he was a ghost. Cosmos knew that came from his time in the French Foreign Legion. A tattoo on his arm was the only mark that distinguished that Garrett had a life before.

He had called to inform Cosmos that he and Lan, the Prime palace's head of security, had recovered Helene Baskov less than an hour before Cosmos planned to leave. She was seriously injured when the van she was being transported in crashed and rolled into a river. Lan had transported her to Baade for immediate medical attention.

"I'm coming with you," Garrett had told Cosmos in a tone that said there would be no arguing after he had relayed the information. "I've seen how strong and fast those bastards are. You need someone to cover your back."

"I have someone," Cosmos responded.

"Let me clarify that. You need someone with a pulse to cover your back. RITA doesn't count," Garrett said dryly. "Have the gear ready for me. I'll be there within two hours."

Cosmos thought about leaving anyway, but realized that Terra's safety was too important to chance failure. With Garrett at his side and covering his back, he would have a better chance of making it out not only with her, but alive. He just didn't plan on the other last minute addition to his team.

"Hey Cosmos, *me siento un poco vulnerable aquí. ¿No podrías haber hecho estas malditas cosas un poco más grande? Creo que tengo un wedgie,*" *Hey Cosmos, I feel a little vulnerable here. Couldn't you have made these damn things a little bigger? I think I have a wedgie.* Rico called out as he pulled at the back of the prototype suit he had put on.

"Damn Rico, what have you been doing?" Garrett said as he came up behind his friend. "The Buns of Steel videos again?"

"Ah man, you are creeping me out," Rico said in a slightly accented voice before he grinned and tried to twist so he could look at his ass. "But I have to admit, this suit makes my ass look good, mi amigo."

Cosmos glanced back, feeling his lips pull up in an amused smile. Rico had turned over the search for Natasha Baskov to his sister Maria. She was working with Brock to find Natasha.

Lan had rejoined them after the healers told him that Helene would recover. Garrett said Lan freaked out when he found out it was Helene and not Natasha in the van but knew he needed to get her help before he could go meet up with Brock and Rico to search for the female he claimed was his mate. Garrett had notified Rico of the recovery immediately and told him to expect Lan. When Rico heard that Garrett was pulling out to help Cosmos, he had handed over the search for Natasha to his sister.

Maria was a tenacious little thing that had a way of seeing things others missed. Rico said it was from their time living on the streets in Madrid. Maria wouldn't stop until she had recovered Natasha. This left him to cover Cosmos' other side.

"I'm telling you, Cosmos," Rico said as he walked up to stand next to Cosmos who had turned back to look out at the ocean in front of them again. "When I first met Mak, I was scared shitless. He is one huge *hombre* but I liked him, even with those scary silver eyes and weird fang thing. After seeing him and the others fight, I was glad they were on our side. Have you thought that kidnapping one of their women might piss them off just a little? I mean, after the way Brock and Lan reacted to Natasha and Helene getting kidnapped, they seem a little on the – I don't know…."

"Deadly side," Garrett suggested as he sat on one of the two prototype flying vehicles Cosmos had on the beach.

"Unforgiving comes to mind," Rico said as he walked over and frowned down at Garrett. "Why do you get to drive? You suck at driving," he grumbled, reaching for one of the helmets on the seat.

"I do not suck at driving," Garrett retorted with a raised eyebrow before he slid his helmet over his head.

"Yes, you do," Rico snorted. "Avery is always complaining about having to clean up after you. She was bitching about how hard it was to make the EC655 you crashed look like it was part of a movie set. She said the next time you crashed a multi-million dollar helicopter into a building, she was going to take it out of your ass."

"I didn't crash it into a building," Garrett replied as he fired up the vehicle. "I set it down on top of it. It just sort of fell apart when I did."

Rico just snorted in disbelief as he slid onto the seat behind Garrett and grabbed the hand grips on the sides. "Don't think this is an invitation, dude. You are too hairy for my tastes."

"Damn, just my luck," Garrett replied into the mic built into his helmet. "Hey, Cosmos! Are you going to stand there all day or are we going to get your girl?"

Cosmos turned toward his own vehicle without saying a word. He had been listening to the other two men as they ribbed with each other, but he was also focusing on the unusual feelings that were bombarding him. The mark on his left palm was burning and tingling.

He thought he vaguely felt another presence in his mind, as if something was brushing against him, trying to get in. He remembered Tink, Hannah, and Tansy all complaining that the Prime warriors wouldn't give them any peace at first. Each one claimed the men could talk to them telepathically. If it was possible for him and Terra to communicate that way, it would help him locate her.

Cosmos slipped the helmet on and brought RITA2 online. The hum of the vehicle under him was deceptive of the power it contained. He brought up a three-dimensional map of the fortress. Within moments, the MFV smoothly lifted off the ground, hovering for a moment before Cosmos twisted the handgrip. The vehicle shot forward, skimming several feet above the waves as it headed out to sea and the island fortress RITA had informed him that Terra had been taken to the night before.

A moment later, Garrett twisted the handgrip on the MFV he and Rico were riding on. A huge grin lit up Garrett's face when he heard Rico's muttered curse as he was thrown backwards. It was only his tight hold on the hand grips that kept him from flying off.

"Damn, I think I'm in love," Garrett said as he gunned the MFV he and Rico were riding and chased after Cosmos.

"Garrett, Rico, there is an entrance to a cave a little over seven meters underwater on the northern face of the cliff. RITA2 has deployed the sensors throughout the building, but not all are online yet due to some interference caused by the security system. The entrance and cavern are both big enough to fit the transports. We will scale the wall up to the fortress. RITA2 is working on taking down the defense systems on that side of the fortress."

"What do you mean working on bringing them down? I thought your damn computer had taken control of the defense and security systems," Garrett growled out.

"What is with the body suits, Cosmos? What do they do? I hope they are waterproof," Rico muttered as his eyes flickered through the displays on the inside screen of his helmet. "There is an opening on the north wall. It looks like a drainage pipe. I think we could fit through it. The sensors there are showing only a moderate security grid. I can get through it."

Cosmos flicked his eyes over to the command screen to give him the same view Rico was seeing. Sure enough, there was a small drainage channel. The bars over it wouldn't be a problem. He looked at the security the sensors were sending back. Rico should be able to take them out. They had seen worse.

"So man, what about the suits?" Rico asked again. "Do they do some kind of super shit?"

Cosmos felt the tug at the corner of his mouth again. This is why he liked the crew he worked with, they were totally unimpressed most of the time with his inventions. When he did invent something really cool, they took it in stride like it was just another toy they would get to play with for a while before they got a chance to try to destroy it.

"You could say that," Cosmos replied. "They make you virtually indestructible against most things. They also have adaptive technology built into them. While we can't fly with them, we can come pretty damn close. RITA2 will help you with the operations. You have the contact lenses in that I gave you?"

"Yes," both men answered at the same time.

"Jinx," Rico said. "I get to drive on the way out."

"Damn," Garrett muttered. "You better do a better job than you did when I let you drive when we were in Morocco."

"I did pretty damn good. I got us out!" Rico snorted. "And, Avery wasn't pissed at me. I got her car back in one piece – almost. There were only a few missing parts."

"And a hell of a lot of dents – on my side of the car," Garrett replied as he flicked through the prototype suit's capabilities. "Damn, Cosmos, this thing has grips that let you walk up walls? What does the invisa-shield do?"

"You'll see," Cosmos replied.

He tilted the MFV he was riding on toward the water. Right before it hit the surface a clear shield formed over the outside of it, covering him in a flexible bubble that shifted so it was streamlined in shape. The shield provided protection and worked automatically depending on the environment or threat.

In this case, it provided protection from the water and because he was attached to the MFV, it was protected as well. He had only tested it a few handful of times in the river along the warehouse and once out at sea. After a few trials and errors, he was able to perfect it. While it looked like a bubble, it was actually made of energy that expanded out from the suit, forming a pocket between the two.

Cosmos grinned when he heard the echoed 'Oh shit!' in his mic as Garrett and Rico followed him. They would be within range of the fortress' scanners in another five meters. He didn't want to take a chance of it picking them up. He guided the MFV downward until he was almost ten meters below the surface. They would be under the scanner and would stay below it all the way to the fortress. Once there, they would be close enough to slip undetected into the underwater cavern. They would leave the MFVs there, swim out, then scale the cliff to the drainage pipe.

"Cosmos, there is a problem," RITA2 suddenly came on over his mic.

"What is it?" Cosmos asked.

"I'm detecting explosions at the fortress and a number of skimmers heading in," RITA2 replied. "The defense systems are failing. Poor DAR is doing the best he can but it would appear there has been an explosion in the primary control room. It has taken out the main power. The attacking forces have destroyed the backup power. Defense shields are failing all over. I don't think you are going to have to worry about going through the drainage pipe. The fortress is under attack."

"Can you tell me who it is and how many?" Cosmos asked.

"I can give you a ballpark. Thank goodness you had me deploy those cute little bugs. Now that DAR has gone down, I have full access to them all now. Give me a second and I'll have the information you are asking about. I'll also see if I can connect to the frequency that those attacking are using so I can pick up what they are planning," RITA2 said anxiously.

"Garrett, Rico, we are going in hot," Cosmos said grimly.

"We heard," Garrett replied in an icy voice. "I hope to hell your weapons can take these bastards. They move like lightning when they want."

"The suit will help compensate for some of that," Cosmos replied. "It won't make us run faster, but if they try to attack, it will stop them – I hope," he added under his breath.

"Great, it's Istanbul all over again," Rico grumbled. "Let's go kick some ass."

"Cosmos, from what I've gathered there are at least forty warriors attacking. They want the females," RITA2 said, worriedly. "I tried to help DAR get back online, but he hasn't responded yet. I can't patch into him to give him a boost. They have landed in the central yard. I detect hand-to-hand combat going on with the few guards at the fortress. I'm afraid they will be quickly overwhelmed. DAR did do a lock down of the section housing the women before he went down, but I've already detected a breach in the outer doorway."

Cosmos!

Cosmos jerked as Terra's voice suddenly filled his head. She sounded both scared and angry. A feeling of completeness filled him as her voice washed through him. It was as if the last missing piece to a puzzle had finally been put into place. He opened his mind to her, reaching to touch her in return.

Terra, tell me what is happening. I'm coming for you. I'm almost there, Cosmos thrust out desperately, hoping that she could hear him.

I heard the guards talking. There are warriors attacking! They have breached the security systems, Terra replied. *I am trapped in the room they put me in.*

Do you know which part of the fortress you are in? RITA2 can send some of the sensors there so I know what to expect. How close are the warriors to you? Cosmos asked in a deceptively calm voice. *Are you safe for the moment?*

I think so, Terra replied, her voice shaking even in his mind. *I am not put in the main part where the other women are being kept. I'm not sure where I am but I know the other females were kept in a different part of the fortress. I heard the witch that is in charge of this prison tell the guards to keep me away from them until I had adjusted.*

Adjusted? Cosmos asked.

A hint of amusement colored Terra's voice as she replied. *I haven't been very cooperative, I'm afraid. I detest the outfit they expected me to put on.*

Good for you, Cosmos chuckled before he sobered. *I'm about twenty minutes out. You keep yourself safe until I get there. I'll have RITA2 give me updates. You focus on staying safe.*

I will. Terra's response fluttered through his mind as if she was thinking of other things as well. *I almost have the lock figured out. I'll have more of a chance if I can get out of this damn cell. There is no way I can hide from anyone in it. And Cosmos…, I knew you would come, thank you.*

You can thank me later, Cosmos growled back. *I promised you I would come and nothing will keep me from getting you out of there. Just to warn you, your father is really on my shit list right now.*

That's okay, Terra snorted. *He's on mine too. Be safe.*

You too, Terra, or you'll know what it feels like to piss me off, Cosmos murmured before he felt her drift away again as Rico's voice echoed in his ear.

"Cosmos, hey man, you there?" Rico asked in a concerned voice.

"Yeah, Rico, go ahead," Cosmos said.

"Does RITA2 have a location lock on your girl?" Rico asked. "And what about the other women? We can't just leave them," Rico said in a steely voice.

"We aren't going to leave them," Garrett said in a cold voice.

Cosmos sighed. "I don't have a fix on her yet, but I'm working on it. She's okay for the moment. She is being held separately from the other women. I'll go after her while you guys help the other women. RITA2 has their location. You heard what she said. There is no sense in stashing the MFVs. We'll travel faster on the surface. Let's go and make sure it is a cleaner escape than Istanbul was," Cosmos added before he shifted the MFV toward the surface.

"Shit, forty to two," Rico muttered. "Not bad odds. We've had worse."

"Yeah, not bad," Garrett agreed wryly. What he didn't add was that those odds weren't against aliens who could move faster and were trained for battle from the time they were in diapers. "Let's go kick some ass."

Chapter 9

Terra worked the panel off the side of the wall with the small tool Mak told her to always carry with her. Her big brother had always looked out for her. Ever since she could remember, he had always had time for her.

When she was seven, he had taken her under his wing, teaching her how to defend herself and how to escape should she ever be taken. When she was eleven, he had given her a special tool that contained a small laser cutting beam, light, and additional blades as a gift. He made her promise to never go anywhere without it.

Out of habit, she had slid the tool into her pocket before she had left Cosmos' home and had not taken it out. That was one of the reasons she refused to change. After her arrival she had been taken to a room where she was instructed to change into the heavy gray gowns the females were expected to wear.

She had refused. She had no intention of changing out of her comfortable blue jeans and cotton blouse that Tilly had given her. If she was to escape, it would be much easier to do so in the pants than the heavy gown.

Lady Mey 'Toc Keila was informed of her refusal. The Grand Dame of the fortress swept in long enough to recite a long list of rules and instructed the guards that Terra was not to be fed until she had complied with the rules. Terra really didn't care what the woman had to say, she didn't plan on being there long enough to care if she missed a few meals.

"Come on," Terra whispered under her breath as the explosions that had begun shaking the fortress minutes ago sounded closer. "Remember to slice through the wires on the right side," she muttered out loud, remembering Mak's instructions.

The panel fell to the floor next to where she was kneeling with a loud clatter. She ignored it as she let the small beam from the laser cut through the wiring. The door to her cell clicked as the lock disengaged. Terra stood up, keeping the small tool in her hand. The laser could be used as a weapon if needed. She cautiously opened the door to her cell and peeked out. She breathed a sigh of relief when she saw the corridor was clear. Slipping out of the room, she looked back and forth. The explosions were coming from the way she was led into the holding area so she figured she would be better off heading in the opposite direction. Running down the long hallway, Terra rounded the corner and almost plowed into Lady Mey 'Toc Keila who was standing in the hallway looking pale and shaken.

"Oh!" Terra squeaked as she skidded to a stop in front of the older woman. "Is there another way out of here?" She demanded when she saw the Grand Dame's eyes widen in surprise.

"What? How…?" Lady Mey 'Toc Keila whispered, looking with dazed eyes at Terra before looking beyond her.

"Is there another way out?" Terra demanded harshly as she heard a loud explosion coming from the direction of her former cell. She gripped the woman's left arm and pulled her further down the corridor, away from the noise.

Lady Mey 'Toc Keila's frightened eyes turned back to Terra. "Yes, but it will only lead you out to the outer walls of the fortress. There is nowhere to escape to," she choked out in terror. "It is better to die than be taken by those savages."

Terra jerked backwards when she saw the older woman raise her right hand that she had hidden in her long skirt. A laser pistol was tightly gripped in the slender white hand. The pistol shook dangerously as she pointed it at Terra.

"I promised to protect the women that were brought here," Lady Mey 'Toc Keila whispered in a trembling voice. "I swore to your father that I would not let anything happen to you. I'm so sorry, Lady Terra."

Terra stumbled back against one of the doors lining the corridor. Shaking her head, she put her hand out in front of her as she stared at the woman in horror. The look of regret in the woman's eyes told Terra there would be no stopping her from her task.

"No, please," Terra begged. "My mate is coming for me. Please… don't."

"It's too late," Lady Mey 'Toc Keila replied just as three warriors burst around the corner, charging at them. "I swore on my life to protect you."

Terra fell backwards as the laser pistol fired. She let out a cry as she felt weightless for a moment before the breath was knocked out of her as she hit the ground.

Lady Mey 'Toc Keila's screams of terror rang in her ears as darkness swallowed her.

* * *

Cosmos pushed the MFV to the max. They were just clearing the wall to the fortress when he felt a wave of terror swamp him. It took a moment before he realized that the terror was not coming from him but from Terra.

Terra! Cosmos silently called out. *What is it?*

Cosmos, Terra called out in desperation. *Lady Mey 'Toc Keila...*

Terra! Cosmos called again when Terra's voice abruptly faded from his mind.

"I've got her, Cosmos," RITA2's voice echoed in his mic. "I was able to patch into the system thanks to those darling little sensors. I'm working on getting DAR back up. He should be online in another twelve minutes. You better move it, though. I don't think he is going to be very happy when he comes back online."

"Where is she, RITA2?" Cosmos asked, setting the MFV down on the upper wall of the fortress.

"I've downloaded a map to her," RITA2 replied. "You may want to hurry. I've sealed the door to the room she is in but there are at least three warriors trying to get into it. The door is re-enforced, thank goodness. From the communications I'm intercepting, they are requesting additional explosives. Hurry, dear."

"Detonate a sensor near them," Cosmos growled as he jumped off the MFV and pulled off his helmet.

He looked down into the interior courtyard. Three large skimmers sat in the center with an additional three hovering above them. Men, locked in battle, fought viciously with each other. It was easy to see those wearing a dark gray uniform were being overwhelmed by those dressed in a wide variety of different clothing.

Loud feminine screams rose from one section of the fortress. Eight dark warriors surrounded a small group of women dressed in long, gray gowns. The women huddled together as the men pushed them towards one of the skimmers. His eyes jerked over to two additional warriors who were struggling to pull another woman toward one of the other skimmers. A loud war cry sounded as a small figure dressed in a colorful gown suddenly attacked one of the men.

Cosmos turned to look at Garrett and Rico as they pulled their helmets off. "Go help those women. I have to get to Terra. She's in trouble. We have twelve minutes and counting to get off this rock before RITA2 gets the defense system back up," Cosmos bit out, turning.

"Hot damn," Garrett said with a grin. "Forty warriors and twelve minutes, I think this is going to be a new record, Rico."

"*Usted y sus registros malditos. Uno de estos días, usted habrá registro de otra persona, mi amigo,*" *You and your damn records. One of these days, you will be someone else's record, my friend,* Rico growled back with a frown as he watched one of the men strike the smaller woman. "That asshole is mine," he added with a nod toward the huge male trying to drag the smaller woman toward the transport.

Rico gripped the unusual pistol Cosmos gave him earlier in his hand as he jumped over a low wall onto a set of stone steps leading down to the center courtyard. Garrett watched his friend for a moment before he followed him. His eyes moved to the center area again, narrowing on the slender figure of the taller woman who fought fiercely against the man still holding onto her.

Yes, he thought savagely, *it was definitely time to kick some ass.*

* * *

Cosmos ran along the upper rampart to the far side. A narrow door sealed the end. Raising his palm upward toward the door as he ran, he sent out a small pulse of energy from his gloved hand. The door exploded inward, ricocheting against the back wall before falling limply to the side.

"Damn, I need to adjust the intensity of this thing," Cosmos muttered as he climbed over the mangled door to the stairs leading down.

"Cosmos, I've detonated one of the sensors. It has pushed the men back for a moment, but I don't think it is going to last long," RITA2 whispered in his ear.

"Why are you whispering?" Cosmos growled out.

"Oh, I just thought it added to the adventure and mood," RITA2 said cheerfully. "In all the movies the heroes are always whispering to each other during a mission."

Cosmos shook his head as he wound his way down the stairs. Only he would get stuck with a computer that was as weird as Tilly – *in a very good way,* he quickly added with a slightly guilty conscience.

He jumped the last couple of steps once he reached the bottom. He stopped as he came to another door. He quickly accessed the sensors in the area.

The corridor leading to Terra was on the other side. Pulling a small tubular device from his waist, he aimed the laser cutter at the metal surrounding the lock. Within seconds, the beam cut a ragged line around it. Cosmos pushed the door open at the same time as he reached out to Terra again.

Terra, Cosmos called out silently. *Honey, I'm almost to you. Can you hear me? We are going to have to move fast. We only have eight minutes to get the hell out of here.*

Cosmos? I'm locked in another room, Terra responded with frustration. *I can't see a thing. The light I have barely cuts through the darkness and I don't want to drain the charge on it.*

I know, sweetheart, Cosmos responded. *RITA2 will be able to open the door with the help of some sensors I've deployed. In just a minute, a charge will destroy the locking mechanism. When it does, you are going to have to move fast. Turn to your left and head straight down the corridor and make a right at the corner. There is a door and stairs leading up to the rampart surrounding the fortress. I have a transport waiting for us. Rico and Garrett are with me. They are trying to help the other women that were taken.*

There are men in the corridor, Terra said fearfully. *I can hear them trying to get in.*

I'll take care of them, Cosmos replied. *You just be ready to run the moment the lock is blown.*

Alright, Terra answered. *Just… just be careful.*

I will, Cosmos promised. *Be ready… now!*

Cosmos rounded the corner on silent feet. There were three warriors in the corridor. Two of the warriors were working on the door leading into the room where Terra was hidden while the other stood over a huddled figure sitting against the wall. He could hear the sobs of the older woman who was begging the men to let her go. Cosmos let out a loud roar, charging at the men just as the sensor inside the locking mechanism of the door exploded with a small pop.

Cosmos aimed the modified laser pistol he had developed using a design similar to the one the Prime warriors had. He fired three quick shots hitting each man in the chest. The pulse of energy knocked the men backwards where they collapsed. The door to the room holding Terra swung open and she tumbled out, almost tripping over the legs of one of the downed warriors.

"Cosmos!" Terra cried out, running toward him.

Cosmos wrapped his arm around Terra's narrow waist, pulling her into him and brushing a hard kiss over her lips before pushing her behind him as four other warriors came into view further down the long corridor. He stepped in front of Terra as one of the warriors raised his arm and fired at him. The energy shield pulsed around both of them.

"Go!" Cosmos demanded. "Get to the transport up on the rampart and get the hell out of here. RITA2 will guide it."

"What about you?" Terra asked, gripping Cosmos' arm.

"Don't worry about me. Go!" Cosmos ordered as two more shots were fired at them. "Now! We only have five minutes left to get the hell out of here before RITA2 turns the defense systems back on."

Terra nodded and stumbled backwards before turning and running. She heard the sound of laser fire behind her and prayed to the Gods that Cosmos would be protected. She gripped the edge of the doorway, turning to watch the men retreat as Cosmos fired on them. Biting her lower lip in indecision, Terra turned reluctantly and began climbing the steps.

* * *

Cosmos let out a curse as another round of fire lit up the shield of his suit. He could see the power levels beginning to drop with each hit. He wanted to follow Terra but he needed to get the old woman curled against the wall up and to safety first. He couldn't leave her defenseless.

Aiming, he fired a couple of shots, forcing the men to duck back behind the corner. Reaching down, he gripped the woman's arm and pulled. He winced when the woman let out a loud screech of terror.

"Chill out, will you! I'm just trying to help you, damn it," Cosmos growled in a low voice when she started fighting him. "You need to get up and move."

"Please don't hurt me," the woman wailed.

"Damn it! I'm trying to save your ass," Cosmos said, yanking her up and shoving her behind him. "Now move your ass or I'm going to knock you out. I'm running low on power and the defense systems will be up again in less than three minutes."

"I have to stay," Lady Mey 'Toc Keila pleaded. "This is my home. I am in charge of protecting the women here."

"You are ...." Cosmos started to say but was cut off by the flash of a warning signal indicating he had less than twenty percent power left in his suit. "Listen, I don't have time to argue with you. If you want to stay, I'll get RITA2 to seal you in one of the rooms until the defense system is back online," Cosmos growled out in frustration as several more shots hit his suit and the power dropped to a dangerous level. "Shit! RITA2, open a damn door then seal it behind her before I get my ass shot."

"On it, honey," RITA2 replied in a cheerful voice. "Second door behind you. Shove her butt in the room and get the hell out of there. DAR is booting up and you have more company approaching."

"More... Damn it all to hell," Cosmos cursed loudly, roughly pushing the old woman through the door that RITA2 had opened. "How many and who the hell are they? Can you dismantle or shut down their systems?"

"Oh, I don't think Dumbass would appreciate that. There are fifteen battle skimmers approaching. J'kar, Borj, Derik, and a host of others are coming in hot and heavy. Something tells me they are not going to be happy to discover you are here anymore than these other guys," RITA2 replied with a deep sigh. "Damn, but they are really something else when they are all protective and angry - even Dumbass is hot."

Cosmos ignored RITA2's observation of the desirability of Prime warriors, especially Terra's dad, and instead gripped several small explosives in the palm of his hand. They weren't powerful enough to do more than stun anyone approaching, but it would give him time to get up the stairs without a bunch of guys shooting at his back. The power of his suit was depleted and unless he could patch into the MFV to recharge it, he was shit-out-of-luck.

Tossing the explosives, he turned and sprinted up the stairs, taking them two at a time. He stumbled as the explosives detonated, but was able to keep his feet under him as he fell against the wall. He pushed off, reaching the top of the stairs in time to see Terra fighting with a couple of warriors who had scaled the wall to the upper rampart. He paused for a brief second, watching in amazement as she twirled around, knocking one warrior off his feet and opening a long slice along the arm of the other warrior who had grabbed her. The moment the warrior released her, she brought her knee up into his groin, bringing him to his knees. The other warrior who had been knocked backwards down several of the stone steps had regained his footing and was preparing to attack her again.

Cosmos charged the man from the side, wrapping his arms around the man's waist as he tackled him. He landed on top of the man and struck him several times, hitting the warrior in the chin, nose, and throat. He was able to stun the man long enough to reach for the pair of wrist cuffs he had on the utility belt around his waist. He quickly slapped the thick band around one wrist before flipping the man over and gripping the man's other wrist.

The warrior fought briefly, but Cosmos let go of the man's arm just long enough to grab a handful of hair and quickly slammed his forehead into the stone floor, taking care of any resistance. He had just immobilized the one he had tackled when he felt his body being lifted as he was grabbed from behind. A moment later he was airborne. His breath left him as he slammed into the low stone wall surrounding the upper part of the fortress.

Cosmos vaguely heard Terra's outraged cry before the shadow of the remaining warrior hovered over him. He fought to regain his breath, searching for his other laser pistol when the man's eyes widened in surprise before rolling back in his head as he collapsed. Terra stood over the inert body holding one of the helmets from the MFV between her hands.

"Take that, you… you jerk! Weak female, my ass," she growled out breathlessly.

Cosmos grinned up at her as he climbed to his feet. "Remind me never to piss you off," he said huskily as he brushed a tender kiss along her lips.

"I hate to put a rush on things, but DAR will be back online in about thirty seconds," RITA2 replied just as an explosion shook the area as one of the hovering skimmers exploded. "Mm, I take that back. He is back online now."

"My father..." Terra cried out as she watched as another one of the skimmers exploded.

"Tell her not to worry, Cosmos," RITA2 replied. "DAR knows not to attack them. I warned him about the incoming skimmers and he knows who the good guys are, not to mention that killing the leader of the planet isn't a good idea."

Cosmos watched two of the skimmers on the ground lift off before rapidly disappearing over the south wall of the fortress. "Why didn't the damn defense system knock those ships out?" Cosmos asked as he turned back around to watch Garrett, Rico, and a taller woman dressed in a long gray gown rush up the stairs.

"He couldn't take a chance with the females on board," RITA2 replied. "His defense protocol is to protect the women. His programming prevents him from harming a female under any circumstance."

Cosmos turned his head and watched as several of the incoming skimmers engaged the two remaining skimmers while three went after the two vessels that had taken off. He looked back as his men reached the top of the rampart and hurried toward him and Terra. Garrett pulled the woman behind him while Rico looked like he was ready to erupt into a Berserker's rage.

"Love the suit, but you need to work on the damn battery life," Garrett snapped out as he pulled the woman closer to him when she tried to pull away.

"Let's get the fuck out of here," Cosmos said, ignoring Garrett's comment. "I'm not going to give Teriff a chance to take Terra again."

"I'm not going," Rico said stubbornly as Cosmos turned toward Terra.

Cosmos looked over his shoulder with a dark frown. "What the fuck do you mean you aren't going? We have to get the hell out of here!"

"I said I'm not going. I'm going after the girl," Rico said, turning away from Cosmos, Terra, Garrett, and the other woman. He grabbed a helmet off the MFV that he and Garrett had arrived on. "I'm taking the MFV."

"Like hell you are, Rico," Garrett growled out, turning to Cosmos. "Open the fucking Gateway and take the women. I'm going with Rico."

"What in the hell is wrong with you two?" Cosmos asked, stunned. "Rico, let Teriff and the others go after the woman."

"I can't," Rico said in a quiet voice as he sat on the MFV and powered it on.

"Why not?" Cosmos asked, exasperated with the two men he trusted the most to follow orders and get a job done.

"This is 'why not'," Rico responded, holding up his left hand. A series of small circles showed clearly in the center of his palm. "I have to go after her."

Cosmos cursed loudly as he watched Rico lift off without another word. "RITA2, you make damn sure that DAR doesn't fire on Rico!" He ordered as he watched the MFV glide over the wall and circle back toward the south and the mainland.

"I have to cover Rico's back," Garrett said, reaching for the helmet in Terra's hand. "I can't let that crazy son-of-a-bitch go off alone. Maria would castrate me if anything happened to him. Take the woman back and keep her safe until I return."

"No!" The woman said, pushing back against Garrett with an angry frown. "I am going."

Garrett looked fierce as he shook his head. "Like hell you are!" He growled out.

The woman smiled nastily as she pulled the laser pistol that had been at his waist up and leveled it at his chest. "Like 'hell' I am. That is my sister they took. I will not be denied."

Cosmos ran his hand through his hair as he looked back and forth between Garrett and the woman then back down to where Teriff was exiting one of the attack skimmers. His breath exploded out of him as he realized exactly what it felt like to be in the middle of a Mexican standoff. He glanced at Terra who was watching with wide-eyed amusement as Garrett and the woman stared at each other.

"Fine!" Cosmos exploded as he looked back down at Teriff who was shooting daggers at him. He handed his helmet to the woman. "I don't know what the fuck is going on but I am taking Terra with me right now. You two cover your asses or I'm going to be sending in Avery and her crew to come get you out and that is going to piss a LOT of men off," he promised as he gripped the portable Gateway device tightly in one hand while he wrapped his other arm around Terra, pulling her against him.

In seconds, a shimmering doorway appeared. Cosmos glanced one more time at Teriff who started forward sharply when he saw the Gateway open between their worlds. His loud roar of rage echoed over the noise far below. Cosmos smiled wickedly before he gave a sharp nod to Teriff in acknowledgement of the challenge the warrior had just issued. Without a backward glance, he pulled Terra through the doorway with him.

Chapter 10

Cosmos paused on the other side of the Gateway, waiting for it to close. The moment it did, he pushed Terra back against the wall of his lab. His lips covered hers in a deep, desperate kiss of relief, hunger, and need.

His hands ran up under the thin T-shirt she wore until they reached her breasts. He groaned when he felt the unbound flesh. He cupped the heavy weights in the palms of his hands, stroking his thumbs over the taut nipples as he ran his lips along her jaw to her neck.

"If you want me to stop, you better tell me now," he muttered hoarsely as he gently nipped her earlobe. "I am going to make love to you, Terra 'Tag Krell Manok. I'm going to claim you as mine and no one, and I mean absolutely no one, is going to take you away from me again," he vowed, pulling back to look down into her eyes.

Terra shuddered as need poured through her body, leaving her shaking. "You're damn right no one will," she whispered as she wrapped her arms around his neck. "I want you, Cosmos Raines – forever."

Cosmos swept Terra up into his arms. He turned and headed toward the stairs leading to the upper level of the lab. He took them two at a time before heading to the set of double doors, securing the room from the rest of the warehouse. He pulled Terra closer as she laid her head against his shoulder and turned her face into his neck.

"RITA, secure the warehouse. I don't want anyone, and I mean anyone – alien or human – getting into it," Cosmos ordered as he headed up the narrow stairway to the second level and his living quarters. "Have RITA2 give you updates on Garrett and Rico and have her help them any way she can," he added as an afterthought.

"Don't you worry, honey," RITA replied with a sigh of contentment. "I'll hold the fort while you claim your mate. My sis is informing Tresa and Tilly that you have Terra. Both of us are monitoring the Gateway so no one will get through without going through us."

Cosmos pushed the door to his bedroom open with his shoulder and released the breath he was holding when he saw the tousled sheets on his king-size bed. His cock was hard as a stone as he thought about what was about to occur. He should have claimed her weeks ago regardless of his promise to her brother. He only hoped the big guy was more understanding than Teriff. If looks could kill, Cosmos was a dead man.

All thought deserted him when Terra reached up and nipped his neck before running her tongue along the vein. A low moan escaped him as he carefully lowered her onto the bed. He followed her when she refused to let him go. Her lips were pure torture as they continued up to his jaw. Her hands tangled in his hair, holding him to her as she rose up enough to rub her breasts against his chest.

"I don't understand what is happening, but I feel like my body is on fire," she whimpered as she continued to run tiny kisses over to the corner of his mouth. "I hurt, Cosmos. What is going on?"

Cosmos chuckled at the confused, breathless question. "It's natural, baby."

Terra pulled back far enough to glare up into Cosmos' eyes. "Well, I don't like it! I don't understand and I want you to make the ache go away," she demanded, looking frustrated.

"Oh, I'm going to make the ache go away," Cosmos promised as he pulled back far enough to reach for the bottom of her shirt. "I don't think you are going to be complaining when I get done."

Terra gasped as Cosmos jerked her shirt over her head. His muttered oath echoed when he saw what his hands had discovered earlier, she wasn't wearing a bra. The rounded mounds swelled as he stared down in awe at them. Her nipples were a dark rosy color. He didn't think twice, his mind was on auto-pilot as his mouth zeroed onto one of the taut tips. He latched onto the rosy peak hungrily, sucking deeply and running his tongue roughly over it.

"Cosmos!" Terra cried out, arching up with a loud gasp. "Oh Gods!"

Cosmos released the swollen tip, turning his head to attack the other one with the same zealous hunger. His hands worked their way down to the button of her jeans. He flicked the button before reaching desperately for the zipper. With a smooth jerk, he had it down and was gripping the sides of her jeans with both hands.

He pulled her jeans and panties down, cursing when they got tangled around the tennis shoes she was wearing. He pulled back, sliding down to the end of the bed. With a quick jerk, he pulled her shoes and socks off. He tossed each one over his shoulder impatiently before he grabbed the end of her jeans and ripped them the rest of the way off. He tossed them onto the floor next to the bed.

His eyes darkened as he took in the beauty of the woman lying in the middle of his bed looking at him with flaming silver eyes. His eyes ran down her slender length, pausing to take in the rapid rise and fall of her chest as she struggled to catch her breath. His eyes moved possessively down, pausing again at the smooth folds between her legs. Terra's legs moved restlessly when she realized where his eyes were focused. Cosmos reached forward, gripping her thighs and forcing her to open for him.

"You don't have any hair here," Cosmos purred as he ran his finger along the silky fold. A smile curved his lips when her thighs fell apart. "I think you like that."

"No, Prime women do not have much body hair except for on our heads," Terra groaned as he continued to stroke her. "I love it, but it is making the ache worse," she whimpered. "Please, I need you to do something."

"With pleasure," Cosmos said.

He straightened up so he could pull the zipper on the prototype suit down. He unstrapped the leather boots and yanked them off before he quickly shrugged out of the bodysuit. Reaching up, he pulled the black T-shirt under it off. He left his boxers on, knowing that if he felt the sensitive skin of his cock brush against her smooth heat he would lose it. He wanted to bring her to pleasure first before he claimed her. Then, they would both experience it.

"You are so beautiful," Terra whispered, devouring Cosmos with her eyes as she reached out to touch his hot flesh.

* * *

Terra shivered as she watched Cosmos strip out of the uniform he was wearing. When he reached up and jerked the black shirt over his head, she couldn't lay still any longer. Something deep inside her demanded that she touch him, taste him, explore his hot flesh. She had never had this burning need before. She had seen males before. Most had been during her training as her father and brothers refused to let her treat the males in the palace.

Still, she had studied the vidcoms and trained on the holographic forms of the male anatomy so she would know what to do should the need ever arise. Nothing prepared her for what she was experiencing. When her mother first talked to her about the desires of a male, she had never explained that she would be overwhelmed with a deep ache to have him possess her.

Terra could feel the heat burning deep in her belly and there was a strange dampness between her legs that she had never experienced before. It was like she ached for Cosmos to connect his body with hers. She knew that was the way males did it. She had never seen it done as there were no vidcoms of the experience, but she knew how their young were created and what needed to be done.

She was a scientist, after all, and it was important to understand the fundamental concept. She had not focused on the reproductive process before as she was more interested in wounds and disease repair. Now, she wished she would have asked Tink, Tilly, and her mother more questions instead of being shy about it.

Her hand trembled as she reached out and touched Cosmos' flat stomach. A fine line of dark hair narrowed down and disappeared under the black silky undershorts that he favored. The front of the silk shorts was tented.

A small smile curved her lips as she recognized the evidence of his need. Her fingers curled along the waistband, intent on pulling it down so she could see him again. She had only caught the brief glance of his cock yesterday in the bathroom and she wanted a chance to explore it more closely.

"Don't," Cosmos strangled voice said sharply. "I won't last if you do. Let me ease the ache for you first. Then… then I'll let you explore."

Terra looked up into his eyes. They were darker than she had ever seen them. His mouth was pressed tightly together, as if he was in pain.

You are hurting, Terra said, reaching out to him in confusion. *These feelings cause you pain?*

Cosmos' soft chuckle echoed in the room as he pressed her back down onto the bed until she was laid out below him. The silver eyes staring up at him were dark with desire, confusion, and worry. He lowered his head until his lips were almost touching hers.

It is a good pain, Cosmos assured her. *You make me feel things I never thought were possible. The moment I saw you I knew I was in trouble. You make me afraid.*

Why? Why do you think I am trouble? How can I make you afraid? Terra asked.

She looked into his eyes as he stared down at her with an intensity that pulled at her soul. She lifted her hands and ran them over his shoulders, down his forearms and back again before she cupped his cheeks between her soft palms.

Why? She breathed out.

I love you, Terra. Cosmos closed his eyes for a second before he responded. He was overwhelmed for a moment at the power of the intimacy at being able to talk to her this way and the feelings it evoked inside him. *You make me feel so much. I'm terrified that something will take that away from me. I need you and that makes me vulnerable.*

Terra didn't know how to reply to such a confession from the amazing man above her. She reacted more out of instinct than knowledge as she pressed her lips to his. Her tongue slipped out to caress the firm lips pressed against hers. When his lips parted, she slipped inside, savoring the taste of him.

I will never let anyone take you from me or me from you, she promised as she deepened the kiss. *Together we will be stronger. You will never be vulnerable because I will stand by your side as you will stand by mine.*

A shudder washed over Cosmos as her passionate pledge swept through him. His arms tightened around her as he took over the kiss. It grew more desperate, wild as their hands tangled - searching and grasping.

Cosmos broke free, sliding down Terra's body. He gripped her hips as he latched onto her left breast again. He suckled on it, relishing the feel of her fingers as they tangled in his hair, pulling his mouth closer as she arched into him. Her legs moved restlessly under him, alternating between wrapping around his waist and opening for him as his fingers moved to the slick folds hiding her womanhood.

Cosmos! Her frantic cry filled his head as she panted, looking up at the ceiling with dazed eyes. *You promised to take the ache away, but it is growing stronger.*

Open for me, sweetheart, Cosmos demanded as he followed his fingers with his mouth.

"Cosmos!" Terra cried out stunned as he opened her to his mouth.

Cosmos groaned as the first taste of Terra swept over his tongue. She was sweet like honey and spicy like cinnamon. She was built slightly different from a human woman. Instead of one clitoris, she had three small ones set in a triangle. He teased the tip of one with his tongue. Her loud cry echoed throughout the room. He leaned forward, sliding a finger deep inside her vagina as he clamped down on the three tiny nubs. A burst of flavor exploded as her body reacted to his touch.

"Damn but you taste good," Cosmos growled as he pulled his finger out and added another. "Come for me, baby."

"Come... where?" Terra panted as she tightly fisted the bed covers in her hands. "Oh Cosmos, I... I..." A low cry that built in intensity echoed as Terra's body tightened before exploding as Cosmos worked her with his fingers and mouth with a hunger that devastated her. "Oh Gods!" She cried out as her body shattered.

Cosmos continued to work his fingers in her slick vaginal channel as he drank deeply. She had unknowingly wrapped her legs around his shoulders and tilted her hips up, pulling him closer so he couldn't escape.

I'm not going anywhere, honey, Cosmos promised her as she continued to explode around him.

I... I... I think I'm dying, she responded weakly.

Cosmos gently pulled Terra's legs from around his shoulders as he pulled away from her. Her hiccupped sob told him she was still locked in the throws of her first orgasm. He quickly shed his boxers, kicking them off as he climbed up over her.

He gripped her thighs and aligned his throbbing cock with her slick channel. He gritted his jaw as he slid the purple bulbous head just inside her slick entrance. Sweat beaded on his forehead as he waited for her to look up at him.

Drowsy eyes opened wide at the first contact of his body slowly pushing forward. "What?" She asked as he pushed a little further into the tight passage. "Oh," she moaned as he pulled back and pushed forward a little deeper. "Yes," she said, raising her hips and wrapping her legs around his waist so her heels dug into his taut ass. "Oh yes," she breathed out.

"Oh fuck," Cosmos groaned.

He leaned over her and surged forward, driving his cock into her as far as he could go and held still as he waited for her body to adjust to his invasion. He crushed her trembling lips to his in a kiss that spoke of the effort it was costing him to control his need to take her hard and fast.

He shuddered as she began moving under him. The feel of her silky flesh fisting him made him want to weep. Never before had he felt such an overwhelming, or primitive desire, to mate. His balls hurt from the fullness. He pulled back slightly, wanting to make sure that he wasn't hurting her. The low growl of distress that escaped her pulled a relieved sigh from him as he pushed forward.

"I want more," she demanded as she gripped his shoulders.

"Who am I to deny you what you want," Cosmos responded through gritted teeth as he began pumping his hips faster.

"Yes," Terra cried out as the feelings she had felt before built deep inside her. She wanted to feel that flood of overwhelming pleasure again. "Like that, but more as well."

"Damn," Cosmos groaned loudly as he rocked faster and harder. "I don't think I'm going to last long."

Terra rocked her hips with him, driving him deeper inside her with each move. The sliding of his cock along the nubs of her womanhood sent waves of heat and pleasure rocketing through her. Each movement of his hips hit nerve-endings she hadn't even been aware of having. She didn't understand why the females of her species were so reluctant to join with their mates if this was what happened.

Yes, there is pain, but it is a pain that is filled with so much pleasure I know I will grow addicted to it, she thought as her eyes fluttered and closed as she connected with Cosmos and what he was feeling.

That was the last thought she had before her body erupted again with a fierceness that rivaled her first orgasm. She arched forward while her head fell back against the soft pillow, her body frozen as it burst apart. She vaguely heard Cosmos' loud groan as his body stilled above hers. The flood of heat as his seed filled her pulled out her orgasm, surpassing the first one and drowning her in wave after wave of ecstasy.

"Terra," Cosmos groaned out as his body pulsed deeply into hers. He let his head fall forward and he pressed a kiss to her exposed neck, his arms wrapped tightly around her body as he held her close. "I love you, my silver-eyed mate."

Terra opened her eyes, staring at the ceiling as he continued to press hot kisses to her neck and pulse deep inside her. Her eyes shimmered with tears as a multitude of feelings bombarded her. She was open to him, feeling everything he felt combined with her own emotions. The love he felt for her was warm, raw, possessive, and primal. She felt the resolve in him to protect her with every fiber in his being. His mind was fascinating. She could feel his focus was on her, yet at the same time, images, calculations, and diagrams of items she could only guess at were flashing through it. It was as if he was going through what weapons he would need to ensure she was kept safe. She could also feel his exhaustion.

"Shush," she whispered as she ran her hands soothingly through his hair. "I am safe with you. Rest. RITA will protect us both," she murmured as exhaustion from a night without sleep and the satiation of their love-making caught up with her. "Sleep, my mate."

Chapter 11

Cosmos smiled as he woke. He didn't open his eyes yet as he wanted to just enjoy the feeling of having Terra wrapped tightly against him. He had woken several hours before and made love to her again, tenderly this time. His whole body felt rested.

He rubbed his chin against the top of Terra's head and released a sigh. A frown creased his brow when another sigh echoed his before the bed dipped beside him. There were two things that registered immediately. First, the sigh did not come from the woman in his arms. Second, the bed was dipping beside him.

His eyes flew open in alarm. When he saw the amused eyes staring down at him, all he wanted to do was pull the covers over his head. Instead, he let out a long groan followed by an even louder curse.

"God damn it, Tilly," Cosmos growled. "Can't you give a guy a break?"

Angus' chuckle from behind Tilly woke Terra, who jerked upright with surprise. Luckily, she kept the sheet tucked around her or Angus would have gotten an eyeful of her lush curves. Unfortunately, the covers were dragged down low over his hips. His cheeks flamed with embarrassment when Tilly's eyes widened in delight.

"Angus," Cosmos snapped looking at the older man with a raised eyebrow.

"Come on, love," Angus replied with a deep laugh. "I think Cosmos and Terra need a few moments alone to get decent."

Tilly sighed again as she rose when Angus put his hand under her arm. "Oh Angus, all of our babies have found their partner."

"Yes, dear," Angus said as he slid his arm around his wife's tiny waist. "Now, how about seeing to your own partner?" he whispered in her ear. "You've been so worried about the kids, I'm beginning to feel a little neglected."

Tilly's eyes lit with amusement as she reached up and pulled Angus' head down so she could kiss him. "I can't have that, now can I?" She responded huskily.

"Enough already," Cosmos groaned out, pulling Terra back down into his arms. "How the hell did the girls survive living in a motor home with you two?"

Angus laughed as he turned his wife toward the bedroom door. "We never said it was easy. Get dressed, Cosmos. You and I need to talk. You have one very unhappy father pacing back and forth, and threatening dire consequences if RITA2 doesn't open up the Gateway for him. I think we need to plan how to deal with him."

"Deal with him," Tilly snorted. "I'll show that overbearing pompous windbag how I deal with anyone who threatens to kill one of my kids. I'll…"

Cosmos sighed in disbelief. "How the hell did you guys get here? I thought I told RITA not to let anyone into the warehouse."

"I had to let her in, sweetheart," RITA responded cheerfully. "She threatened to cut access to DAR if I didn't *and* she promised to work on a hologram program for me and my sis. How could I refuse? I did tell Dumbass that he could take a long hike off a short bridge. Well, I didn't, but RITA2 did."

Terra giggled as she rolled over to look at Cosmos. "Good morning," she whispered brushing a kiss across his pursed lips. "I like waking up next to you," she added in a surprised tone.

Cosmos looked up into her shining eyes and couldn't stop the smile that curved his lips. "Why do you sound so surprised?" He asked curiously.

"I am trying to understand why the females of my world are told that such things are not to be enjoyed," Terra admitted with a puzzled frown. "I mean, it is amazing!"

Cosmos shook his head and chuckled. "I think it is pretty amazing too," he said huskily as he pulled her down to kiss her again.

"Oh!" A voice came from the doorway.

Cosmos let his head fall back to the pillow before he turned his head and glared at the doorway. Tink was standing in the center of it looking wide-eyed at Cosmos and Terra. She wasn't the only one. J'kar was glaring at Cosmos with a savage look.

"Mom said to tell you to get a move on. Teriff and Tresa are coming," Tink said brightly. Her eyes danced with merriment as she saw Cosmos wrap his arms protectively around Terra. "Don't worry about Teriff. He'll just blow out a lot of hot air. J'kar can tell you he didn't like me at first either. Isn't that right, honey?" Tink added, looking up at the dark face of her mate.

"No, but that was different," J'kar growled out, looking at Cosmos with a frown.

"Knock it off," Tink said, turning and putting her hands on J'kar's chest and pushing him back. "He loves her. Just like you love me. Remember, you aren't supposed to get me upset – I'm pregnant."

Cosmos looked at the petite, rounded figure of his best friend. She barely came up to the Prime warrior's chest but she was backing him up as if she were twice his size. He opened his mouth to ask her to close the door behind her but she must have known as she grabbed the doorknob and pulled it with her as they exited his bedroom.

Terra let her forehead drop down and rest against Cosmos. "I like her," she said with a grin before the smile died. "I will not let my father send me back to that place."

"I won't let him send you away from me," Cosmos promised. "You belong to me now."

The smile that had died returned briefly. "I like that. You belong to me as well."

"Let's get a shower and dressed before anyone else shows up. RITA, you and I need to have a serious talk when this is over about following orders!" Cosmos called out as he rolled out of bed and scooped Terra in his arms.

"I've turned the sensors for your room off so you two can have some privacy. Mums the word, darling,"

RITA replied with a laugh. "Besides, Tilly is scarier than you are any day."

Cosmos snorted as he walked into his bathroom and gave the command for the water to turn on in the shower. He gently set Terra down before opening the glass doors. He stepped in and reached for her hand as she stepped in behind him.

"Can I wash you?" He asked as he brushed her hair back away from her face.

"If you do, we may not get out of the shower," Terra said with a shake of her head. "Then, we will have all of them in here with us, knowing Tilly and my father. That is not something I would appreciate."

"Me either," Cosmos admitted.

A shudder escaped him at the idea of having to deal with two such powerful personalities while not wearing a stitch of clothing. With a rueful shake of his head, he reached for the shampoo. He was ready to kick them all the hell out of his warehouse, lock it down, disable RITA, and say to hell with everything and everyone but the beautiful nymph in the shower with him.

Life is bloody not fair sometimes, he thought with regret as he watched the soap bubbles run down his mate's spine to the curve of her ass.

I totally agree with you on that one, Terra replied wistfully.

* * *

"She stays!" Cosmos growled out, rising from the table and slamming his palms flat against the table.

"She's mine and no one, including you, is going to take her away from me."

"We'll see about that," Teriff snarled as he rose as well to face off across the table from where Cosmos and Terra were sitting.

Tilly and Angus sat on one end while J'kar and Tink sat on the other. Tresa sat quietly in the chair next to Teriff. She laid a hand on Teriff's forearm while Terra tried to calm Cosmos.

They had been arguing for the last forty-five minutes. Teriff wanted to take Terra home. He promised he would not send her back to the fortress. In fact, all the women who had been held there, save Lady Mey 'Toc Keila, three warriors, and those taken, had been moved to the palace. Gant, Brawn, and Bullet had vowed to keep the women safe, even from members of their own clans.

Derik, Core, and Hendrik were still in pursuit of one of the vessels that had departed. The vessels had split up. According to the readings they were able to get from DAR before the vessels departed, one had eight women aboard while the other only had one. The decision was made to rescue as many as they could. That meant following the transport containing the eight women.

Mak remained back at the palace at Tansy's side as she was still unconscious and Borj was overseeing everything at the palace while Teriff was gone. Borj refused to let his pregnant mate out of his sight. Hannah sat by Tansy's side, keeping watch over her sister during the short periods of time Mak disappeared to take care of business.

None of them talked about Mak's demand for Right of Justice against the men who had harmed Tansy. The healers had healed the man named Craig that Teriff brought back. Mak had dealt justice out this morning to him in the arena.

Now, his middle son searched for the man named Drew who had betrayed Tansy and killed her first mate. These were just a few of the reasons Teriff did not want his precious daughter anywhere near a world where men were responsible for so much pain.

"You think human males are such savages, but what the hell do you call locking your own daughter up in a prison? What about those men who attacked it? What the hell do you think they would have done to Terra if they had gotten their hands on her?" Cosmos fired back. "I'll see you in hell before I let you put her in another place like that."

"I…," Teriff began before Tresa spoke up in a stern voice.

"Teriff, sit down," she ordered.

Teriff looked down in shocked surprise at the tight expression on his mate's face. He sat down more out of surprise at her speaking to him in such a tone than because she ordered him to sit.

He drew in a deep breath and looked at the faces around the table. Tresa, Tilly, Terra, and Tink all looked at him with a stubborn expression that did not bode well for him. Even Angus had a look of disappointment on his face as he stared back at him.

Teriff flushed before looking at his oldest son's face. J'kar looked like he was torn between wanting to support the need to take Terra back and the knowledge that if he did, Tink would not be happy. From the grimace on J'kar's face, Tink must have shared her opinion with her mate.

"Tresa," Teriff began, turning to look at his lovely mate.

"No! You listen," Tresa interrupted him before taking a deep breath to calm herself. "Cosmos is Terra's mate," she began gently. "He has proven that he can protect her. He is right. You should never have sent Terra to the Isle of the Chosen, but I am glad that you did," she paused when she heard the other women gasp. Tresa shook her head as she glanced from her mate's stunned face to those of the others sitting around the table.

"If he had not sent her there, the other women would still be there. The fortress was needed long ago, but not now. It took an incident like this to prove that women should not be taken from their clans and housed like they were animals. The time has passed when it was necessary to treat us like we are property. Terra has the right to accept the mate the Gods have given her. The mating rite is complete. She and Cosmos are bound. There will be no more talk of taking her away," Tresa said firmly, looking back into the eyes of her mate. "Would you deny her what you and our sons have?"

Teriff swallowed down the protest as he listened to his mate's words. With a sigh of resignation, he shook his head. "No, I would not deny her," he admitted reluctantly before turning to glare at Cosmos who had sunk down into his chair as well. "You better keep her safe – and happy!"

Cosmos nodded in relief as he gripped Terra's hand tightly between both of his. "I promise I will keep her safe, do everything I can to make her happy, and love her with every fiber of my being," he vowed.

"One more thing," Teriff said gruffly looking at Tilly instead of Cosmos this time.

"What?" Tilly asked, startled as the heated silver gaze turned on her. "What did I do?"

"Besides stir up every male Prime warrior over the age of mating, hack into our computer system, and stick your nose in Baade business?" Teriff asked with a wry grin.

"Yes, well besides all of that," Tilly said with a blush.

"Could you please ask RITA2 to turn on the hot water and release the locking mechanisms on the doors? It is becoming as you would say 'a pain in my ass'."

Tilly's delighted laughter filled the air. "RITA?" Tilly called out.

A loud sigh echoed throughout the room. "I'm on it. Does this mean we can't call him Dumbass anymore?"

"Yes, dear," Tilly chuckled.

"I'll talk to my sis and let her know things are cool now. Oh, Cosmos, Avery is on her way in. I'll let her tell you what she has found," RITA informed them.

"I'm off to work on the hologram program. RITA2 promised to introduce me to a system called FRED. He sounds awesome."

"I've heard that name before," J'kar murmured with a frown, trying to remember where it was. His eyes grew wide when he did. "Oh, Gods, no!"

"What's the matter?" Angus asked, looking at J'kar as the huge warrior paled slightly.

J'kar looked at his father then Tilly and Angus in horror as Tink burst out laughing. "FRED is the name RITA2 gave the computer aboard my warship."

Avery walked into the room to discover a table full of laughter. She shook her head, wondering what the hell was going on. She had to wait almost five minutes before anyone even noticed that she was standing in the doorway watching them. The moment they saw her, they burst into laughter again.

It is going to be a long day at this rate, Avery thought with a disgusted shake of her head.

Chapter 12

"From what I've been able to find out so far, it looks like your big friend was hit at least three times. The last bullet took him down. If you look at the surveillance footage I was able to get, it looks like two of Avilov's men took him. I swear they were going to erase his ass, but if you look here...," Avery paused the video she had on display in the living room. "This one realized he wasn't from the local star system."

Avery used the pointer on the remote to point out where the taller of the two men stopped the shorter one from putting a bullet in Merrick's brain. The man kneeled down next to Merrick, lifting his lip. The way the man fell back spoke volumes. The man stood and spoke to the shorter man who made a call. Five minutes later, a van pulled up and they watched as several men jumped out and loaded Merrick into the back. A few minutes later the van disappeared.

"Were you able to get a license number on the van?" Cosmos asked as he stood next to the couch.

Avery shook her head. "Not yet. There are a lot of surveillance cameras in Washington, D. C. I was able to get a fix on the two men who shot him and one other. They are on Avilov's payroll. I'm working on tracking them now. Avilov is a paranoid son-of-a-bitch and so are most of the men who work for him," Avery explained. "I should have more in a couple of days. I have Rose and Trudy on it. They are sifting through the information with RITA's help, but like I said, there is a hell of a lot of video to go through. I think you can bet your latest invention that Avilov is aware that he is dealing with more than he was expecting by now."

"What do you plan to do?" Teriff asked as he leaned back against the wall, staring at the stilled picture of the warrior who lay bleeding on the ground.

Avery's eyebrow rose as she calmly looked at the huge Prime leader. "I'm going to find him and contain the situation. That's what I do. I have never failed and I have a bonus riding on not failing this time," she answered with a mysterious grin that sent a shiver down Teriff's spine.

Cosmos thought it best not to mention that the bonus was a visit to a certain Prime warrior who made the mistake of catching the interest of a very dangerous and very determined human female. Cosmos cleared his throat as his mind worked on the avenues available to them in order to find both Merrick and Avilov. Not for the first time, he had a moment of regret at not thinking through the Gateway he had invented.

Do you regret meeting me? Terra asked, refusing to look at Cosmos. *Do you regret my brother saving the life of your friend?* She added, trying to shut him out by focusing on the screen as Avery continued to answer her father's questions.

Never, Cosmos responded, turning to look down at Terra. His heart melted when she refused to look at him. *Terra, look at me.*

Terra reluctantly turned to stare up at Cosmos. Her jaw was set in determination as she refused to let him see how badly he hurt her with that thought. She would not grovel to any man, including Cosmos.

Cosmos knelt in front of Terra, taking her hands gently in his own. He held her gaze, willing her to open her mind fully to him. It took several long moments before she opened to him again.

I love you. I have no regrets about it. I just regret that things have turned out this way. If I had been more prepared, perhaps I could have saved the men who died. Perhaps I could have saved Merrick from being taken, Cosmos said tenderly. *But if it meant never meeting you, I would not change a thing. You are my world now. Never doubt that. I love you more than life itself.*

Together we are stronger, Terra said, raising her hand to tenderly touch his cheek. *There will always be 'perhaps' in life. It is the Gods who place the obstacles in front of us. It is how we deal with those obstacles that lead our path in life.*

Cosmos pressed a hot kiss into her palm. *I stopped believing in God a long time ago,* he admitted.

Then just believe that we are stronger as one and perhaps things worked out the way they were supposed to, she replied lightly.

Kismet? Cosmos responded.

Kiss me, Terra responded with a nod.

Cosmos chuckled, knowing she did not realize the definition of the word he said, instead misinterpreting it. *With pleasure,* he replied, brushing a kiss over her lips.

"What do you think, Cosmos?" Avery asked dryly. "I think it is time to confront the Runt. She must be on to Avilov. Did you know that she was at the warehouse the other night? She is damn lucky she wasn't killed.

I've had my eye on her since she was eleven and hacked into CRI, sniffing to see if you were legit."

Cosmos leaned back on his heels and stood up, turning to look at Avery, who was watching him with a raised eyebrow. "I didn't know she was there the other night. We need to see if she saw anything as well. Other than that, I think asking her to join our corporation would be an excellent idea. The Runt is one of the best hackers in the world according to RITA who has blocked her from hacking into CRI at least a dozen different times. I think she will enjoy the challenge of bringing Avilov's kingdom down. She must know something, otherwise she wouldn't have been at the warehouse. Just make sure she has adequate protection. She will become a target the minute things start closing down. Hell, she's only fifteen and even the government has been trying to find her for the past four years."

Avery shook her head, amazed that Cosmos could follow the conversation. She knew damn well something else was going on from the look on his face as he knelt in front of the alien woman who had caught his fancy. It was like he was talking with her, but his mouth never moved.

"She might try to run again. It took me eight months to find her this last time. She is going to shit a brick when she finds out we have known about her since she hacked into your corporation. Things have been hard for her since that no-good father of hers died. I love the fact that we are going to get her out of that shit hole that she has been hiding in. Did you know that she has been homeless and living in an abandoned building along the Navy Yard in D.C. since her dad died two months ago? I've tried to help her out, but she is a skittish little thing."

Cosmos frowned at Avery. "Why didn't you tell me sooner? I would have done something."

"Not with this one," Avery said dryly. "She makes a thoroughbred look like a pack pony. She's fast, distrustful, and can disappear down the rabbit's hole in the blink of an eye. I am going to have to take a team in to capture her as it is and I guarantee she won't come without a fight."

"This girl was at the warehouse the other night?" Teriff asked with sudden interest. "Where was she? Are you sure she was outside the warehouse where we found Tansy?"

"I'm sure. We've had an agent on her since we found her again two months ago. Bert is one of our older team members. He is less threatening and was standing on a corner down the road from where Knapp took Tansy. He said he saw her heading toward the warehouse earlier. She disappeared for a little while, but reappeared shortly after the fireworks began. He said he saw her running away from it. Someone was chasing her, but she knows those warehouses like the back of her hand and was able to slip away. The only way he can keep track of her is when she brings him a meal once a day from the local food bank or he catches a glimpse of her as she sneaks around. He, Walker, and Briggs take shifts. She steers clear of the other two, but took a shine to Bert," Avery explained. "Why?"

Teriff looked thoughtful for a moment before he shrugged his shoulders. "Just curious if the human might have seen something," he responded lightly before he turned to slip his hand into Tresa's slender one. "We must return to our world. Tilly, are you and Angus staying or returning?"

"Returning," Angus said immediately. "We need to make sure Tansy will recover. We only came here because I was concerned when you said you were going to challenge Cosmos. I didn't want my wife getting in the middle of your fight and I guarantee you, she would have."

"You're damn right I would have," Tilly snorted.

"I would have been right beside you, Tilly," Tresa chuckled as she squeezed her mate's hand.

"Me too," Terra added.

J'kar turned and covered Tink's mouth with his hand when she opened her mouth to add her support. "Gods, then Tink would have been there too," J'kar said before he hissed loudly and jerked his hand away from the set of teeth that had bit him.

Tink licked her lips. "You're damn right I would have. Like mother, like daughter, right, mom?" She asked with a huge smile.

J'kar groaned as he felt his cock respond to his tiny mate's bite. "Let's go home. I have a better idea of what you can do with that mouth of yours than bite me."

Tink flushed and looked wide-eyed at him. "You shouldn't say things like that in front of our parents!" She hissed out under her breath.

"I think that is an excellent idea," Teriff added with a grin as he jerked Tresa against his hard body. "Since I can't kill Cosmos, I need to work off my aggression in the bedroom."

"TMI, Teriff," Cosmos said dryly, turning to Avery. "Do what you have to. I trust your judgment."

Avery nodded before she shook her head. "Damn, I think there might be something in the water. I've never seen a hornier bunch of people in my life. I'm out of here since I have to wait before I can do anything about it."

Cosmos rolled his eyes as Terra giggled and stood to press her body against his. "TMI, Avery. TMI."

* * *

"Are you alright?" Terra asked later that evening as they lay together in Cosmos' big bed. "What did my father say to you before he left?"

Cosmos pulled Terra closer to his body. He never realized how much he missed having the place to himself until all the others left. Well, with the exception of Terra. He loved the feel of her in his arms. He loved it even more when he was buried deep inside her.

"I can hear your thoughts," Terra said, amused as she saw his eyes darken. "Now tell me what father said."

Cosmos grimaced as his mind swept back to his conversation with Teriff, or he should say, Teriff's list of threats against him. The Prime leader had taken him to the side to have a brief 'talk' before he left. The talk consisted of all the ways he was going to rip Cosmos apart while keeping him alive if anything happened to his daughter.

The fact that he was accenting his points with a very sharp blade in his hand didn't help. Tresa had finally rolled her eyes and guided her mate away, talking quietly to him in an effort to calm his reluctance to leave Terra behind. Cosmos remembered flushing when he saw Teriff jerk to a stop and turn to stare at Terra's stomach before he raised dazed eyes up to meet his. Cosmos' stomach flipped as he turned to look at Terra who was smiling at her mother with one of those secret smiles only women seemed to understand.

Cosmos took a deep breath before he shook his head to dismiss that thought. He supposed it was possible that Terra could be pregnant. They hadn't used any type of protection, but there was no way to tell if she was after just one day – was there? His stomach rolled at the thought of what it would mean to have a baby. Hell, there was so much going on and they had just gotten together. It would be crazy to throw a baby into the mix with everything else going on – wouldn't it?

"I'm not," Terra said quietly. "Your seed has not taken root in my womb. A Prime woman knows when she is with child from all the research I have done and the information I have obtained from the few females who have conceived. It might not even be possible for us to have a child," she whispered sadly.

"What do you mean – it might not be possible? As far as I know I don't have any problems with, you know – that. Do you know if you have any problems?

I mean, it doesn't matter to me. I mean, it does, but it doesn't change how I feel about you. I love *you*, Terra. Whether we have kids or not won't change that," Cosmos said, leaning up on one elbow to look down at her. He tenderly brushed her hair back from her face. "I promised your father that I would protect you and do everything in my power to make you happy. I also promised him I would never place you in danger. If it is dangerous for you to have a child, then I'll make sure we don't have any. It is you that is important."

Tears welled up in her eyes as his words sunk in. "Is that all he said to you?" She asked.

Cosmos smiled tenderly down at her, resting his palm against her cheek. "Well, and the fact that he was going to rip me into little pieces and make sure that I felt it if anything did happen to you," he said with a crooked grin.

Terra gave a short chuckle before she just gazed at him for a moment. "There is no reason that I cannot have a child. It is just – Prime males inject a female with a chemical that helps prepare them for mating. It normally takes several injections of the chemical before a female's body accepts his seed. I do not know if I will be able to conceive without the chemical. Nothing like this has ever happened before – the mating between a Prime female and a male from another species," Terra explained quietly.

In that instant, Cosmos felt the difference between their species greater than ever before. The knowledge that he might be the reason they could not have children, that his being human might prevent Terra from having a fulfilling life, shook him to the very core of his being.

All his life he had been different from other people. He had been better than others in many things. He had definitely been smarter and more successful, so the knowledge that he might be lacking was a new concept to him. He fell back against the pillows and stared blankly up at the ceiling, his mind swirling as he ran through all possible solutions to fix this problem.

"NO!" Terra said harshly, sitting up and straddling his waist so he had to look at her. "You are not deficient. You are the smartest, strongest, handsomest, most noble man I have ever known besides my father and brothers. There is nothing I would change about you. I love you, just the way you are and I would never wish for another," she said fiercely. "Do you understand me? I love *you* just the way you are!" She waited a moment before she rolled her eyes when she felt his cock jerk under her ass. "I think your body knows it anyway," she muttered as she started to roll off him.

"Oh no, you don't," Cosmos said huskily. "I think I need a little more convincing. How much did you say you love me?"

"You are incorrigible," Terra giggled as she leaned down over him, letting her breasts brush against his chest.

"But you love me," he responded, shifting her down until his cock was aligned with her heated core. He groaned loudly as she slowly impaled herself on his throbbing shaft. "We'll figure out how to recreate the mating chemical if we find out we can't have kids without it. Together we can do anything."

"Together," Terra breathed out as she began riding him.

Chapter 13

Avilov slammed the cell phone against the wall in rage. It had been four weeks since the night at the warehouse. He had lost over fifty of his best men and several important contacts within the U.S. government.

On top of that, his accounts had been hacked into and all of his funding from his illicit businesses had been seized and given to charities around the world. He suspected that even his contact with the Vice President of the United States had been compromised. His legitimate businesses were being seized by governments around the world or the stock prices had dropped so far as to make the companies practically worthless. He was having to dip into his hidden reserve funds. He knew who was behind it. Cosmos Raines and the creatures he had helping him.

Avilov stared at the screen on his computer. An image of the male his men had captured stared back at him with cold, deadly, flaming silver eyes. He needed to know where in the hell Cosmos had gotten the man. He was not human. All the tests the doctors at his testing facility had conducted proved that he was not from Earth. But where in the hell was he from? That was the billion dollar question.

He was furious because the facility in Oregon where he planned on shipping the male had been seized by federal agents. The doctors studying him had barely had time to move him from the Washington State facility before he was discovered. Now they were taking him to a small facility they had set up in California. It didn't have any of the equipment they needed and was not even a true research lab. It was basically just a converted office building where they had rented a section of the basement to house the male until a better facility could be obtained.

Avilov clicked an icon on the desktop of the small computer to open the current news from around the world that had been delivered to him. The laptop wasn't even hooked to the Internet. Everything he had was brought in on a flash drive and triple checked by his security team before he placed it in the small computer he was using. He had to go off the grid after several close calls.

The first few weeks had been a nightmare as he tried to liquidate as much as he could before it was seized. He barely stayed one step ahead of the agents from around the world seeking him. Hell, he barely stayed one step ahead of the other mob bosses looking to kill him.

They were furious that he had not only placed information about them on the disk that was stolen but had led government forces around the world to their doorsteps. He currently had a fifteen million dollar bounty on his head, preferably with him being brought in dead. Only his closest men knew where he was and even then he didn't trust them. He looked around the sparsely decorated former World War II bunker he had taken refuge in. He was in the middle of Siberia locked in an underground frozen crypt.

"Sir," a deep voice spoke behind him.

Avilov turned with a hand in his pocket, gripping the Makarov pistol as he did. Afon stared at him with cold eyes. He and Afon had become acquainted with each other when Avilov literally plucked the man off the streets of Moscow when Afon was just fifteen years old. Afon already had a reputation for being deadly, but he lacked power and money. Avilov gave him both in exchange for loyalty. So far, Afon had never shown that his loyalty was waning.

"Afon," Avilov acknowledged him with a nod. "Do you have the transportation ready, and have the other men been given their orders?" Avilov asked, turning just far enough to flip through the current documents he had requested on the man he was going to be visiting in Prague. "I don't want you going with them. You will remain with me," he ordered, looking up sharply to make sure Afon understood.

Afon bowed his head in acknowledgment of the order. "I have the team ready to go in after Raines. They have their orders to capture him alive. They have also been ordered to procure any equipment that he has. I've kept everything classified and no electronic dispatches have been sent," Afon said in an emotionless voice. "I have also secured transportation to Prague for us."

"When does the team leave?" Avilov asked coldly.

"They leave tonight. They will not attack until I give the order. I determined it would be best for your untimely death to be announced first. Also, it has been agreed that more information was needed before the team moved in. We need to understand what capabilities the silver-eyed man we are holding has. We also need information on the security system Raines has installed. It would help make the strike more likely to be successful. I have instructed the Team Lead to study the target and notify me of his findings before engaging Raines."

Avilov frowned as he brought up the World News headlines that had been downloaded for him. The announcement that the Vice President of the United States had suffered a deadly stroke and died two days ago chilled him to the bone. The man had been fifty-six and in perfect health, according to his latest medical exam three months ago.

"Sir, when you are ready," Afon said quietly. "We should leave immediately."

Avilov looked up at the man standing before him and had a feeling the trip was not going to be a comfortable one. Avilov nodded and waved his hand to let Afon know that he would be ready to leave shortly. He needed to look over the information he had one more time on the plastic surgeon he had an appointment with and wanted to read the article on the Vice President. He wanted to make sure the surgeon was the best.

His eyes drifted back to the news headline, only this time they drifted to the picture below. There was an article on Cosmos Raines and his current charity funding. A savage gleam glittered in Avilov's eyes before he slammed the lid to the laptop closed in anger and frustration.

Cosmos Raines is a dead man, Avilov thought savagely. *He will spill his secrets before he dies, but he will die.*

* * *

Terra leaned over Cosmos' shoulder to study the information he was looking at on the computer screen. He was going over the information that had been obtained from the files Tansy had stolen. He knew the President was aware of it. J'kar had told him of their visit with the President.

He and his brothers had been frustrated with their mates when they insisted on accompanying him, his brothers, and their father to see the human leader just a week after Tansy regained consciousness. Mak had been beside himself with worry for his mate. She was still weak from her injuries and exhaustion, but determined to go on her own. Mak had tried to get her to let him and Borj handle it, but she just rolled her eyes and told him either she was going with him or she was going alone, but she was going.

Cosmos shook his head and wished he had been a fly on the wall when Tilly and her clan along with a bunch of big ass alien warriors suddenly walked out of a shimmering doorway into the Oval Office like they were out visiting a neighbor. That would have been an awesome sight, especially when Teriff introduced himself as a 'dickhead'. He was just glad that the President had been receptive to listening to them instead of panicking and calling in the military.

As far as he could tell, Askew Thomas hadn't mentioned his unusual visitors to anyone outside of his inner-circle. Avery had informed him shortly after the Presidential visit that there was an elite group of agents looking for a man with unusual characteristics. The only reason she knew was their paths had crossed on more than one occasion during her own search. She informed Cosmos that she had the agents covered should they discover something before she did. Trudy and Rose had narrowed the search to California at this point. Unfortunately, California was a big state with a huge population.

Personally, Cosmos hadn't been surprised in the least bit about the sudden death of the VP almost four months ago. After he had read the information about what the man had been up to and who he was in cahoots with, Cosmos would have killed the man himself. The VP had been responsible for countless deaths world-wide, some directly, according to the report.

It was the additional information that Cosmos was working on right now. The governments were going after the long list of names of the other organized crime bosses. He wasn't interested in those others right now.

He would let the governments do their thing. He would send in teams to take out the ones they missed or couldn't get. No, right now he was more interested in proving whether the newest report was accurate or not. His gut was telling him it wasn't. When he had read that Avilov had been killed in a car bombing by one of his former associates yesterday morning in Paris, Cosmos had been skeptical. Yes, he knew Avilov's former buddies had put out a huge bounty for his head, but something just didn't ring true. He wanted to see the body parts and analyze their DNA. Until he had concrete proof, he would go on the theory that it was a set up to get the heat off of Avilov's back.

"Is that the man you were looking for?" Terra pointed out over his shoulder as a picture of Afon Dolinski popped up on the screen.

Cosmos turned his head and brushed his lips across hers. "Yep, that's him. He is Avilov's right-hand man. If we find him, we find Avilov. He won't be far from him. The reports say only one man was in the vehicle. There should have been two if it was Avilov because he never went anywhere without him glued to his side. The thing is, Dolinski would never have gotten into any vehicle that he had not personally inspected or had total control over."

"It's been over four months since Avilov disappeared and there has been nothing on him. Most of his associates have been apprehended or their funding has been cut off. All of Avilov's assets have been frozen or seized. Isn't it possible that this man could have abandoned him?" Terra asked, scooting over to sit in the rolling chair next to him.

Cosmos' eyes softened as she pulled her long legs up into the seat and wrapped her arms around them. Her bare toes peeked out from under the long sweatpants she was wearing. He would never get tired of looking at her. The last four and a half months had been incredible. When they weren't working on finding Avilov or helping Avery locate Merrick, they were spending time learning about each other.

He knew her mind was as sharp as his and her curiosity was insatiable. Terra had supported the response team when Natasha had been rescued a little over a week after her kidnapping. She had provided medical support to the injured woman. Lan had taken Natasha back to Baade once she was stable for additional medical attention and to recuperate.

Natasha had been in bad shape by the time Maria and Lan had located where she was being held. They had barely made it in time to save not only her but Helene. Helene had gone in after her sister unbeknownst to Cosmos. He thought she was safe back on Baade until a very irritated Prime warrior showed up demanding to know the location of Lan and Maria.

Brock discovered Helene had escaped back to Earth with RITA2's help shortly after Lan had returned to take his place in the search for Natasha. RITA explained her 'sis' just wanted to help Helene out since she was so distressed about her missing sister. She had no idea that the feisty Russian was Brock's mate.

Helene had taken out a good portion of the men who had taken her sister by the time Brock, Lan, and Maria had shown up. Maria later reported that the group of men that had taken Natasha had been a part of an initial coalition between Avilov and another mob boss. It appeared the mob boss had taken a fancy to Natasha and wanted her brought to him. Cosmos was glad they were down to just one missing member now.

"It's possible Dolinski deserted him, but I doubt it. It doesn't fit with his profile," Cosmos said, reaching over to pull Terra's chair closer to his. He smiled when she squealed as the chair rolled across the concrete floor. "Have I told you how much I love you today?" He asked huskily, turning so they were facing each other.

Terra shook her head and smiled. "Only about fifty times. But I'm not complaining," she added teasingly.

"Cosmos, sweetheart. I'm sorry to break up your intimate moment, but your folks are calling," RITA's cheerful voice sounded over the sound system.

Cosmos lowered his head with a groan. He had only talked to them a couple of times over the last four months. They had been in Hong Kong working on a huge project, and except for a few brief conversations he hadn't had much time to ask more than how the project was going and how they were doing. He tried to contact them at least once a month knowing that both of his parents lost track of time when they were in the middle of something. He had always been the glue that kept them together. They weren't bad parents, just single minded when they were working on something, which was almost always.

Raising his head and releasing his breath, he looked into Terra's eyes. She had a supportive, if teasing, smile on her face. They had talked about how he was going to introduce her to them. He was still stuck on the part where he said, 'Hey mom - dad, I'd like you to meet my mate. She's an alien.' Yeah, that just didn't sound like something you told your parents over the phone.

"Patch them through, RITA," Cosmos called out before he grinned at Terra. "Maybe I could ask them to take a few days off and we could fly to Hong Kong and meet up with them."

"That would be wonderful," she said, nervously biting her lip.

"They'll love you," he assured her just as his mother's voice came over the speaker.

"Cos... Cosmos," his mother said in a trembling voice.

Cosmos knew immediately that something was wrong. He could hear the fear in her voice. His head jerked around toward the monitor and to the picture of the man standing next to Afon Dolinski. The man's cold eyes stared silently back at him. Dread clawed at his stomach as he realized he was right – Avilov was not only alive, but the son-of-a-bitch was declaring war on Cosmos.

Chapter 14

Cosmos typed in a command for RITA to trace the call and record it. A quick flash across the screen showed she was already on it. Cosmos took a deep, steady breath, even though his heart was pounding.

"Hi Mom, how are you?" Cosmos asked casually as his fingers flew across the keyboard.

"She is not doing too well, Mr. Raines," a slightly accented voice smoothly replied. "It would appear that she and your father do not care for their current accommodations. A shame, don't you think?"

"What do you want, Avilov?" Cosmos demanded, not even bothering to pretend he didn't know who was behind the call.

Avilov's cold chuckle sent shivers down Cosmos' spine. "I want information, Mr. Raines. I have something of yours and I want to know where it came from. I thought to ask your parents for help, but it would appear they were blissfully unaware of your little experiment and your new friend. Unfortunately, I didn't believe them at first."

"You son-of-a-bitch, I'll kill you if you hurt them," Cosmos snarled out. "I'll fucking rip your heart out and shove it down your throat."

Avilov laughed again. "I believe you really think you could kill someone, but I've studied you, Mr. Raines. You are too much like your father. You like to keep your head in your inventions and your eyes on the pretty ladies, including the one by your side now. Such beauty, much like your mother. It is a shame about your father. I'm sure he was wishing he could have protected her as she watched him die."

Cosmos' hands trembled as he gripped the desk in front of him. "Mom?" Cosmos called out hoarsely.

"He killed him, Cosmos," his mother cried. "Your dad… he killed him," she sobbed out.

"Your mother will join your father, but not as quickly if you are not in the following location by midnight tomorrow night," Avilov said coldly. "Do not try anything, Mr. Raines, or I will send her to you piece by piece."

Cosmos sat frozen as the connection ended. Terra reached over with a trembling hand to touch his shoulder, but he jerked away, standing up and walking over to the railing looking over the initial Gateway. His fingers turned white as he gripped the railing, wishing fervently that it was Avilov's neck instead.

Cosmos? Terra called softly.

Grief raged through Cosmos as he thought about his quiet, eccentric father who loved to tinker on things that would make the world a better place. He closed his eyes as he fought the pain swamping him, knowing that he was the reason his kind-hearted father was dead. He hadn't even taken the time the last couple of months to see his parents much less talk to them for more than a few minutes.

He turned, opening eyes that burned with tears that he refused to let fall. He had brought this darkness to his family, he would end it. He would get his mother away from Avilov and he would kill him.

"Together!" Terra said sharply, standing up and slowly walking toward him. "You are not to blame for this. The man who did it is responsible. Together, we will stop him."

Cosmos shook his head. "Not this time, Terra. I need to do this without worrying about you. I need..." He paused to take a deep breath. "I'll get her out of there. I need you back on Baade with your father and brothers. I have to know you are safe. I'll send my mom through the Gateway to you. She'll need... she'll need support. She has never spent a night away from him. Hell, he even slept on the damn floor when I was born so they could be together," he choked out.

"Cosmos," Terra said, reaching up to touch his cheek. She ignored the hurt when he turned his face away from her touch. "Talk to my father. He can help. We are one now. If you die, so do I. You must understand that our bond links our lives together. It is not like your world where your mother will live on. Our joining is a connection of the soul, mind, and body."

Cosmos turned back to look at Terra. The quiet resolve and compassion in her eyes was his undoing. He didn't resist when she wound her arms around his waist and held him tightly against her warm body. Lowering his head until it was buried in her hair, he wrapped his arms around her. His body trembled as silent tears coursed down his cheeks, dampening her hair and neck. She held him close as pain and sorrow swept through him. He felt her inside of him, soothing his soul with her calm strength. After several long minutes he pulled back and looked down at her with a heavy heart.

"I need to ask your dad a favor," Cosmos choked out.

"He and my brothers will not let you fight alone," she assured him tenderly. "And my mother, the other women, and I will be there for your mother."

"Thank you," Cosmos said hoarsely.

"There is no need to thank me," Terra replied tenderly. "I love you, Cosmos Raines. You are a good man with a good heart. Never forget that. Your mother and father would be proud to know what you do for your world. Never doubt that."

Cosmos' eyes filled with sorrow at the mention of his father. "He'll never know now."

"I bet you he already knew," Terra murmured. "Let us go. We do not have much time."

"Fortunately, Avilov has no idea that we can be there quicker than he expects traveling through the Gateway. I need to get a few things together. Be ready to go in twenty minutes," Cosmos said as his eyes hardened with determination. "RITA, I want the location of that son-of-a-bitch and every ounce of information, including any surrounding surveillance video, downloaded to your sister by the time we leave."

"I'm on it, Cosmos," RITA said quietly. "I'll do what I can remotely. I'm sorry for your loss. I really liked your dad."

Cosmos paused as he turned toward the lower level and the lab he had below this one where he kept his prototype equipment. He paused, pushing the grief behind the wall he had built years ago. His mind was racing as he thought of what he would need to take.

"Thanks, RITA," Cosmos said in a steely voice. "Let's move."

* * *

Avilov nodded to the man holding the sobbing mother of Cosmos Raines. Her dead husband lay at an awkward angle on the floor of the warehouse where he had fallen after Avilov ordered Frazer, one of the new men he had hired, to shoot the man. Avilov had been furious at the man's insistence that he and his wife knew nothing of aliens or his son's inventions.

"Take her to a room and lock her in," Avilov said, turning away. "Get someone to dump the body," he started to say before a malicious smile curved his lips. "On second thought, string it up. I want Raines to see it. That should loosen his tongue. If it doesn't, his mother will join her husband."

Afon nodded. He barked out a few sharp commands and two of the men with them quickly moved to take the body of Adam Raines. His eyes followed the man who looked nothing like he did four months ago.

The visit to the plastic surgeon along with his weight loss, change in hair color and contact lenses made Avilov a totally different man. That was how they were able to travel to Hong Kong to meet up with the contacts Afon had waiting for them.

"Do you want me to give the signal for the Team Leader to move in on Raines?" Afon asked quietly. "He will not be prepared for an attack now and will be vulnerable due to the news of his father and mother."

Avilov looked at Afon and shook his head. "No. I don't want to take a chance of Raines getting hurt. He will come to me. Have your men go in after he leaves. I want the girl captured alive in case having his mother is not enough of an incentive. I also want any equipment they find delivered to the warehouse in Washington, D.C."

"What should I tell the doctor holding the silver-eyed man?" Afon asked. "Should we terminate him? The doctor has grown frustrated as the man continues to resist."

Avilov scowled. He was down to one doctor and three men thanks to that alien. The man had either killed or run off the other doctors and security personnel. Avilov had ordered the ones that ran terminated. Unfortunately, Afon had not been able to find replacements yet. They had to move the bastard a half dozen times in the past four and a half months. They were currently using a private clinic for patients with mental disorders outside of Reno, Nevada.

"I've told you before, until we know where he came from and what he is capable of, he is to be kept alive," Avilov snapped.

Afon's mouth tightened, but he refrained from voicing his opinion. Personally, he felt the huge bastard should have been immediately terminated. The alien was too unpredictable to be allowed to remain alive.

Even sedated, he was dangerous as the last phone call Afon received proved. The man had been heavily injected with sedatives and had still managed to kill a doctor and two of his men before they were finally able to restrain him. Now, he was locked in a re-enforced cell and chained at his wrists, waist, and ankles.

"Yes, sir," Afon responded with a bow. "I'll let the Team Leader know to move in the moment Raines has departed the warehouse."

"That is all," Avilov said dismissively as he turned away.

He waited until Afon had walked away before he headed up the stairs to the room that he had converted to his private quarters. He caught a glimpse of his reflection in the glass windows that lined the walkway. He was no longer the dark-haired, handsome man he had been before. Now, silver hair and wrinkles creased a face that should have shown a much younger man. Once he had what he wanted he would find another surgeon to restore his good looks. For now, he would hide in plain sight as an old man.

A crooked smile curved his lips as he thought of the beauty that Cosmos had been living with the past four months. He only had a few blurry pictures of her, but even that did not hide her soft glowing skin or her rich dark hair. He might just let Raines live long enough to watch as he enjoyed the delicate beauty.

Chapter 15

"Cosmos?" RITA called out.

Cosmos was busy assembling a collection of weapons that he would need to rescue his mother. He needed to be careful as he did not want any of the prototype devices to fall into Avilov or anyone else's hands. The world was not ready for many of the things he had invented.

His eyes moved to the large vessel that he was in the process of building. The huge black hull was made of a new material he had developed. The craft was designed to transport a pilot and a small three-man crew into hostile areas. It was designed for stealth, speed, maneuverability, and protection against enemy fire. The odd shaped hull looked like something out of a Science Fiction or Comic Book movie.

Or, a Baade reproduction battle skimmer, Cosmos thought distractedly.

"What is it, RITA?" Cosmos asked as he turned to focus back on what he was doing.

"I've been keeping a perimeter check of the warehouse and I think we might have trouble coming. All my calculations are showing a ninety-nine percent chance there is something going on," she replied.

Cosmos frowned, running his hand over the back of his neck. "What makes you think that? Avilov knows I'm coming to him. There is no reason for him to send in a team to get me."

"I have a higher than normal concentration of strangers converging around the warehouse. I've been monitoring the incoming traffic, but it hasn't varied greatly over the past few months until an hour ago when four vans and two SUVs parked along the back street about three blocks down from the warehouse," RITA said cautiously. "I know Avilov is expecting you, but something isn't right. I've checked his location and it is in a warehouse based in Hong Kong's Tsim Sha Tsui District. The warehouse is located off of Cheong Wan Road. I've accessed all the video surveillance in the area and uploaded it to RITA2. You were right about Dolinski. He is there."

Cosmos leaned against the table in front of him and lowered his head, closing his eyes as he tried to clear his mind and think like Avilov. The man wanted him, there was no doubt about that, but he wanted something else too. Why would he demand Cosmos travel to him if he was sending a team into his warehouse after the fact?

I have something of yours and I want to know where it came from. The echo of Avilov's voice resonated through Cosmos' mind as he picked up on key sentences from the conversation. His eyes snapped open when he remembered one sentence in particular. *You like to keep your head in your inventions and your eyes on the pretty ladies, including the one by your side now.*

"SHIT! That bastard has had someone casing the warehouse all this time," Cosmos cursed under his breath. "RITA, I need you to contact Avery. Tell her I need an advance assault team STAT! That bastard is going to attack the warehouse and try to take Terra and the Gateway while I'm gone."

"That would explain the unusual activity," RITA said. "But, why not try to take you too?"

Cosmos shook his head at the man's audacity. "Because he wants me alive and the last group he sent in to kill me missed. He knows I have help and I'll fight. If he can bring me to him by using my mother then he controls the situation and he believes it will leave Terra and the warehouse defenseless."

RITA snorted. "That just shows how stupid he is then if he thinks you wouldn't have one of the most advanced security systems in the world in place," she responded. "Avery has alerted Jason. His team is the closest to you. I'm sending him the information now. It will take them four hours to get here though. Oh, and she wanted me to let you know Runt has disappeared again. She said, quote 'I'm going to wring that scrawny brat's neck when I catch her again'."

Cosmos closed his eyes as he realized the fastest way to get them here was to use the Gateway. It would mean more people knowing about it. Jason was relatively new to his team, but he was a good man. Garrett had vouched for him and Garrett never vouched for anyone.

The more he thought about it, the more he realized that there was a faint similarity between Garrett and Jason. Hell, the last thing he needed was things getting more complicated. If that similarity meant they were related, he didn't want to think what would happen when Jason realized Garrett was off chasing bogies on an alien planet.

"RITA, tell Jason to get prepared, but not to deploy until I give him the command," Cosmos ordered, opening his eyes.

Cosmos gathered the prototype suit he had used to save Terra. He draped it over his arm. He couldn't afford to take much else. He could deactivate the suit remotely using the contact lenses he wore to control it if it became evident he would not make it out alive.

It would take years for anyone to re-engineer the material and it would still be worthless without RITA and the technology of the contact lenses. He gathered his utility belt that contained a few cleverly engineered hooks, explosives, and blades before he reached for the small box of sensors. He would deploy the bug sensors to give him more Intel inside the warehouse and help pinpoint the location of his mother – and his father's body. He would not leave his father's body behind.

Turning, he headed back upstairs, calling out an order to RITA to open the hidden elevator. Stepping into the small circular tube, he reached out to Terra. She was waiting patiently for him. He smiled when she opened to him and he realized that she was aware of everything he had been doing, including his conversation with RITA.

I can't keep any secrets from you, can I? He teased before sobering. *I want you to stay with your mom and Tilly when I go after Avilov.*

I know, but you also know that is not possible. If you are injured, I can help. I will be there for your mother as well, she responded in a tone that said there would be no arguing.

Have I ever told you that you are one stubborn female? Cosmos responded lightly.

That is a good thing, my mate. You need someone who is as stubborn as you are. I will meet you back in the lab.

Cosmos' head fell back against the wall of the elevator briefly as he brought up memories of his last conversation with his father. They had only talked for a few minutes, but it was the words that they both said that pulled at him. They had talked business; his father had shared the excitement of their newest discovery and how their presentation in Japan had gone over so well that they had been invited to Hong Kong.

The conversation was normal except for his dad's last words. He hadn't thought too much about it until now. Rerunning that conversation now in his head shook him. It was almost like his dad had known that it might be their last conversation.

"You know, Cosmos, I don't tell you as often as I should but I want you to know that I am very proud of you and the work you do. I know you think I don't pay attention, but what you are doing is making a huge difference to the world and I'm not talking about the charities that you support or your inventions. I'm talking about the people you help and the things that you do that no one but a handful of people know about," Adam Raines had said quietly. "I want you to know I'm proud to call you my son and that I love you very much. I always have. You have been a blessing to your mother and me. I know if anything ever happened to me, you would be there for her."

Cosmos remembered his chuckle of embarrassment at his dad's words. "Hell, dad, you're still young. You and mom have another fifty years to go. How about I fly out to Hong Kong in a couple of weeks and we get together for dinner? I have a few things that I'm working on but I should be able to hop over."

"I'd like that, son. It's been a while since we've seen you," his dad had responded hesitantly. "I miss you, son."

"I miss you too. Give mom a kiss and hug for me. I'll contact you in a week or so to let you know exactly when I will be there," Cosmos had replied absently as he had been working on new information that he had just received from Avery. "Talk to you later."

"Love you, son," his father had said before they had ended the call.

Cosmos' eyes glittered with tears as he stared blankly at the light in the elevator. "I love you too, dad," he whispered as the door to the elevator slid open.

Chapter 16

Cosmos followed Terra and Brock down the long corridor to her father's office. He could feel Terra's unease as they got closer as her memory of the last time she was in the room surfaced. He slid his arm around her waist and gave her a gentle squeeze.

You are not the only one who cannot keep anything secret, she sent out to him with a wave of warmth that showed her appreciation for his touch.

I think your father has finally accepted me. If not, his new grandbabies have kept him too busy to fret, Cosmos responded.

Brock told me Tansy is pregnant as well and Hannah is due any day, Terra said with a small smile. *He said my father is enjoying being a 'Grand' father to Tink and J'kar's twins. He can barely keep his hands off them. Brock said he is threatening every warrior he comes across to keep their sons away from the girls. They are just now learning how to crawl!*

Once this is done, I hope they won't be the only ones he has trouble keeping his hands off of, Cosmos replied.

"What?" Terra asked, startled, tripping slightly as his words sunk in.

Cosmos nodded briefly at Brock, who turned to look at them with an inquisitive expression when they stopped suddenly in the corridor outside of the office. He turned to look back at Terra who was staring up at him with wide eyes. He tenderly brushed her hair back from her face.

"I want us to try to have a child if it is possible," Cosmos said quietly. "When this is over, I want to see if we can recreate the mating chemical – that is, if that is what you want," he added with a sudden look of uncertainty.

Terra's eyes glimmered with unshed tears. She threw her arms around his neck, holding him close as her body shook with emotion. When she felt like she was a little more in control, she pulled back far enough to brush a soft kiss across his lips.

"I love you, Cosmos Raines," she murmured. "There is nothing more in the world that would make me happier than to have your child."

Cosmos' eyes softened as he stared down at the incredible woman standing in front of him. "Have I ever told you how much I love you?"

Terra raised her hand and caressed his cheek. "How about you show me how much later?"

Cosmos turned his head and pressed a kiss into her palm. "With pleasure."

The sound of a throat clearing brought them both back to reality. Turning, Cosmos nodded solemnly to the huge warrior. Brock's lips curved up at the corner to indicate he understood the situation. He had already informed both of them that RITA2 had notified them of the situation back on Earth and recognized the pain etched in Cosmos' face.

Turning, Brock nodded to the two Prime warriors standing guard outside of Teriff's office. One of the guards spoke briefly into his comlink before he opened the door. Brock stepped through, followed by Cosmos and Terra.

A dark scowl crossed Brock's face at the same time as he muttered an even darker oath. "What the hell do you think you are doing here?" He demanded when he saw the petite female with short blond hair streaked with blue sitting in a plush chair near the window.

"Что это похоже, дорогая? Я здесь, чтобы поддержать космоса. Он спас моих родителей и моих братьев. Я не покинет его в случае необходимости." *What does it look like, sweetheart? I am here to support Cosmos. He saved my parents and my brothers. I will not desert him in his time of need.* Helene responded with a raised eyebrow.

"English," Brock growled. "You know my translator is not set for your language yet."

Helene laughed in delight. "I know. But, I also know that it drives you nuts, so how can I resist?" She responded with a mischievous grin. "I will go. I owe Cosmos much for what he has done for my family."

Brock clenched his fists at his side. The crazy Russian female was going to drive him insane. She was always doing things she shouldn't. He glared at her as she smiled innocently at him, as if she was unaware of the conflicted feelings coursing through him.

His eyes jerked to her sister, Natasha, who was sitting back on the couch. Lan stood protectively over her with his hand on her shoulder. Even with the sunlight shining through the window, he could see how pale and thin she was. Her captivity had taken a lot out of the slender woman. Natasha's eyes dropped to where her hands were folded on her lap. Lan leaned over and murmured softly in her ear. Natasha looked at him briefly before she shook her head and looked out the window instead.

Cosmos watched as Brock walked over to stand behind the chair where Helene was sitting before turning to look at the others in the room. His throat closed as he took in Terra's father and brothers standing ready along with Helene and Brock.

His eyes widened when he paused on the much smaller figure standing near the window. Angus Bell looked at Cosmos for a moment before he straightened his shoulders, crossed his arms, and gave Cosmos a brief nod. The look of determination on the face of the normally placid husband, father, and writer showed he was not going to stand aside while Ava Raines was in trouble.

* * *

Teriff looked at those gathered in his office. His eyes dwelled briefly on his daughter's face. Her eyes shimmered with love, grief, and hope. He bowed his head just enough to let her know that he heard her unspoken plea for help.

His heart was heavy as he thought of Ava Raines' loss. He had listened to the Bell women talk of Cosmos over the past several months and his respect for the male had grown the more he learned about him. All he had to do was look at Terra to know his daughter was happy.

Cosmos stood next to her with a protective arm wrapped around her waist. The male looked pale but composed. There was a cold calm that spoke of a true warrior under the deceptively boyish appearance.

"It is time to declare war on the human male who has caused so much grief," Teriff announced. "The man has taken Cosmos parents, killing his father and leaving his mother not only without her mate for protection, but threatening to kill her as well."

"I have already demanded the Right of Justice against him for his attack on my mate," Mak said, straightening up from where he was leaning against the back wall.

"Mak," Tansy said, laying her hand on the huge warrior's arm. "I don't give a damn about justice. I just want the asshole dead."

Mak glared at his mate before his eyes softened. "I will not allow you to go on this mission with us," he said quietly.

Tansy rolled her eyes. "You couldn't stop me if I wanted to go," she said dryly, ignoring his soft growl of protest. "That said – no, I will not be going. I still tire easily, I'm pregnant, and I would be a weak link to all of you as you would spend more time trying to protect me than attacking Avilov and his men. But, that does not mean I can't be a part of the planning or know what is going on. I know Avilov better than anyone. I was his 'girlfriend', after all, before I tried to kill him," she added, drawing another menacing growl from her mate.

Borj nodded. "That is true, Mak. With respect, Tansy, I would be beholden to you if you would stay close to my mate while we are gone," he asked quietly.

"Tilly and mother will be with her, but I would like for someone of your experience to also be close by."

"No problem, Borj," Tansy said with a smile. "I've been protecting my big sis for a long time and don't plan on stopping now," she added, ignoring Mak's muttered threats to tie her up when he got her back home again.

J'kar stood next to his father with his arms crossed over his massive chest. "Tink said she was heading over to your and Hannah's home with Tilly and mother when I talked to her earlier," he told Borj. "She will take the girls there. I have assigned extra guards to protect them during our absence."

Teriff nodded and turned to look at Cosmos who had been quietly listening to everything. "You have information about the area? There will be eight – nine of us," Teriff corrected with a frown of disapproval as he looked at Terra. "Lan, you will remain and have a team ready in case something goes wrong. I will…" Teriff broke off when the comlink on his desk signaled an incoming message. The guard outside the door alerted him that there were additional visitors at the door.

Everyone turned to watch as the door opened. Core, Hendrik, Brawn, Bullet, and Gant walked through it followed by Derik, who looked tired as he quietly slipped behind Cosmos and Terra. Core's face was dark as his eyes swept around the room, noting all the warriors gathered before turning to look suspiciously at Teriff.

"What is the meaning of this?" Teriff demanded as the warriors stopped just inside the door.

Core scowled at Teriff. "I was told to report to your office as were the others. I think I have the right to demand what the meaning of this is more so than you," he growled out.

Terra's soft gasp echoed throughout the room, drawing everyone's attention to the middle of the room where a glowing shape was slowly forming. The apparition was fuzzy at first before it slowly became almost solid-looking.

"Holy shit, it's a ghost!" Tansy said, moving instinctively in front of Mak in an effort to protect him.

Mak snarled and picked Tansy up gently by the waist and set her behind him. He glared at her for a fraction of a second before he turned and positioned himself in front of her. Tansy grimaced when he snapped at her to stay put when she tried to get around him so she could see the figure better.

"What?" She retorted. "It's a habit to be up front."

"Well, break it!" Mak bit out in frustration. "I protect you, not the other way around from now on."

"Whatever!" Tansy snorted as her eyes widened as the figure became clearer. "Holy hell. It's Grandma Bell come back to haunt us!"

"Mom?" Angus whispered, pushing his glasses up onto his nose as he stared at the apparition of his mother.

The peal of husky laughter echoed in the room. "No, honey. It's me, RITA2," the figure said as it turned to look at Cosmos with a mischievous grin. "I called the boys in. RITA and I wanted to make sure you had some kick-ass help. I saw what they did at the fortress. These bad boys have enough muscle to take on half of Hong Kong."

Chapter 17

After the uproar and subsequent fascination of finding out RITA2 had discovered a way to create a three-dimensional holographic image of herself, the meeting progressed fairly quickly. Core and the other warriors quickly sobered when they were given the information about what was happening. The knowledge that the man was also responsible for Merrick's disappearance and probably knew of his location helped.

Core explained briefly that they were able to rescue five women that were taken. Hendrik then spoke up, explaining that three of the women had discovered their bond mates among the men who had taken them. The other men were turned over to their clans for discipline.

"What of the other skimmer that my men were pursuing?" Cosmos asked, concerned with the lack of information about Rico and Garrett.

RITA2's lush figure turned, drawing the attention of all the men. It didn't help that she was wearing a 1920's flapper dress that swirled with beads, and showed off ample breasts and a set of stunning legs.

"Down boys, I'm just an image," RITA2 giggled.

"But what an image," Brawn muttered as his eyes flickered back and forth, watching the fringed hem giving out peeks of slender thighs.

Angus cleared his throat. "That is my mom – I mean – oh hell. Couldn't you have picked a different image?" He grumbled. "This brings back memories of all my friends wanting a date with my 'sister'! Do you know what it was like having to explain it was my mom they were eyeing?"

RITA2 chuckled. "You poor baby. It was either this or Tilly, and RITA is working on that one. Now, to answer your question, Cosmos, I lost contact with Garrett and Rico about ten hours ago. The MFV's power was depleted. The solar cells should be charging now. They had landed in a sparsely covered tundra to the north. It's a good thing those damn suits you created are environmentally controlled or they would be freezing their asses off."

Hendrik grimaced. "Those responsible must be from my clan then. It will be difficult for your men to survive where my clan lives. It is best to forget the female. The warriors who took her will not release her. They will kill your men first before they do that."

Cosmos' mouth tightened. "My men will not leave her. They are more adaptable than you realize. Why would your men kidnap a defenseless woman?" He asked, his heart wrenching as he thought of his own mother's terror right now.

Hendrik shook his head in remorse. "My people are getting desperate. There are few females in my clan. Few can tolerate the ice and snow for long periods of time. The men grow restless as they become more desperate."

"*Его люди должны посетить Россию в течение зимы, не так ли Наташа? Женщины там не только показать ему, как жить в холодную погоду, но удар их высокомерным ослов думая, что они не могли справиться с этим.*" His men need to visit Russia during *the winter, isn't that right, Natasha? The women there would not only show him how to live in cold weather, but kick their arrogant asses for thinking they couldn't handle it,* Helene said dryly to her sister.

A ghost of a smile curved Natasha's lips as she looked at her sister. *"∂a,"* *Yes.* Natasha answered softly.

"English," Brock growled out in frustration as he rubbed Helene's shoulder. "Please."

"She was just pointing out that Hendrik's men were looking in the wrong place if they wanted women who could handle their climate. They need to visit a few of the northern climates on Earth. Russia, Norway, Iceland, Greenland, Canada, and Alaska are just a few. From my readings of the planet, it isn't that much different. Hell, even the scientists living in Antarctica live in a harsher environment than Hendrik's clan," RITA2 replied, looking at her nails that were switching through a variety of brilliant colors and nail designs.

Hendrik's eyes widened, then narrowed as he looked at Helene with a speculative look. Brock moved out from where he was standing behind Helene and emitted a low, challenging growl at the look. His hand moved to the short laser sword at his side.

"She is mine," he warned the huge Northern clan leader.

"But there are others?" Hendrik asked with a grim smile.

"Brock – Hendrik!" Teriff's sharp voice broke through the tense standoff between the two men. "Hendrik, I will discuss ways to help your clan after we rescue Cosmos' mother and get Merrick back," he paused a moment before he placed his hand over his heart. "You have my word."

Hendrik broke eye contact with Brock so he could look at Teriff. The Prime Leader's face showed no hint of deception. Hendrik took a step back and bowed his head in acknowledgement.

"Agreed," he said heavily before he turned to look at Cosmos. "What is your plan of attack on this human? And do I get to kill?" He asked with a sharp-tooth grin. "I am feeling my own frustrations at not having a mate and need to work off some of it."

Cosmos straightened up and looked around the room. "There are two situations going down. Avilov, who is in Hong Kong, has murdered my... father, and has my mother as a hostage. According to the preliminary information I have, he has almost forty men with him at the warehouse where he has taken my parents. I want to bring both of them home," he said heavily, looking around at the men listening. "The second situation is the warehouse I call home and where I have my labs. Avilov has a team ready to infiltrate it the moment I leave. He wants not only my equipment but he wants Terra as well."

Teriff's eyes flashed in fury at the mention of the man wanting to harm his daughter. "Bullet and Gant will take those approaching your warehouse while the rest of us go after your parents."

Cosmos shook his head. "I have a team that can take care of my place. The problem is getting them there in time. I have less than sixteen hours to be in Hong Kong and I need Avilov to think I'm en-route so his people need to see me leave the warehouse. I'll use the Gateway to transport back to here then to Hong Kong so I can get a better idea and plan of attack. I want the team coming after me to see Terra sending me off. The moment I leave, she will transport back here and wait for me. RITA and my team can handle Avilov's team in Maine. They will be good, but I guarantee not as dangerous as the group in Hong Kong. I think it best if we have all the warriors we can there," he explained quietly. "Avilov has a man named Afon Dolinski. He is extremely dangerous. He would keep his best, most dangerous men close to his boss."

"I will go to your warehouse to help your men," Derik said quietly from the corner where he had been standing. "It is best to have at least one Prime warrior there. We cannot take a chance of your team failing and Avilov taking possession of the Gateway."

Teriff looked at his youngest son. He had become quieter, more withdrawn, yet focused over the past few months. He had confronted him about what happened that night at the warehouse, but all Derik would say was that he had killed two of the men in the alley but the third person he was chasing had escaped.

"Agreed," Teriff said with a reluctant nod. His son was no longer a boy but a warrior.

Cosmos turned to look at Derik with a nod of thanks before looking back at Teriff. "I need to use the Gateway to bring my team in, otherwise they won't make it in time."

"They can be trusted?" Teriff asked with a frown at the idea of so many human males in his world at one time. It was bad enough that he had two of them here without his knowledge until just a few minutes ago. "I do not want them to have a portable device."

"They won't, and they can be trusted," Cosmos assured him. He turned and looked at Terra who had been standing silently beside him, his island of strength in the storm that was threatening to consume him. "Let's get going. I want to bring my family home."

Teriff stepped out from around the desk he had been standing behind. He placed his hand on Cosmos' shoulder and squeezed it. Cosmos looked in the flaming eyes and saw the resolve in them.

"Your mother will be brought here," Teriff ordered quietly. "She will not be without family."

Cosmos' throat closed up at the solemn promise. "Thank you," he replied quietly before turning toward the door. "RITA2, lock on Jason's position."

"All set, honey," RITA2 replied. "Good luck and be safe."

Chapter 18

"I think that went better than you were expecting," Terra said softly as she watched Jason and Derik talking quietly while Jason pointed out where his men would set up in preparation for the attack on the warehouse.

They were making the final arrangements before they left for Baade then Hong Kong. Cosmos, Terra, and Derik had appeared in the staging room in the New York compound a little less than an hour ago. To say they had startled the shit out of Jason and his men would be an understatement. It was only the fact that Jason was well versed in Cosmos' penchant for inventions that stopped him from opening fire. That didn't mean that the three of them weren't greeted with enough firepower to start World War III.

It had taken several minutes before the men relaxed their guard. The fact that both Derik and Terra had flaming silver eyes blazing and were trying to protect Cosmos, Derik better than Terra as Cosmos kept pushing her behind him, didn't help much until Cosmos barked out an order to lower their arms.

"Don't you ever stand between me and a gun again," Cosmos said sternly before he brushed a kiss to soften his words. "You scared the hell out of me. I thought you were going to rip Jason a new one."

"He should not point things at you that can hurt you, then," she responded, looking back over at the handsome man.

"Handsome?" Cosmos asked with a raised eyebrow. "You think he's handsome?"

Terra flushed and looked up into the dark burning eyes glowering down at her. "You are not jealous, are you?" She asked in surprise. "He is handsome but I am only observing that because it is true, not because I have any desire to be with him."

Cosmos glared at one of the soldiers walking by who was studying Terra with more than a little interest. He pulled her down the corridor toward his bedroom. Too much had happened and he needed a moment alone with her. Shutting the door to his room, he pulled her close to him.

He buried his face in her neck, holding her tightly against his taut length. "I can't deal with them looking at you like that right now and I definitely can't deal with you looking back, even in curiosity. I'm terrified of losing you, Terra. You should be back on your world with your mom and Tilly and the others, not in the middle of a firefight that is guaranteed to be nasty," he said hoarsely, pulling back to look back down at her. "I can't stand the thought that something could happen to you."

Terra pressed her lips briefly against his. "Then think about what we are going to do when this is over. Think only of being safe so we can try to make that baby you promised me. Think of settling your mother into my world. Think only about staying safe for me. I will not come in until it is safe. I have promised you that. RITA will let me know what is going on. She will monitor the sensors that you deploy. I will be there if you need me to help remove your mother and provide medical attention."

"You promise?" Cosmos asked as indecision scorched his insides.

"I promise to remain safe until I am needed," Terra said. "Believe it or not, Mak did a very good job of training me to defend myself. I am also stronger and faster than you."

"Really?" Cosmos said skeptically.

Terra grinned and moved so fast Cosmos was left startled as he felt his feet leave the ground where they had been standing by the door. His breath left him when he found himself lying on his back in the middle of his bed with Terra straddling him. He was still trying to catch his breath as she leaned over him.

"Really," she assured him.

"Damn!" Cosmos muttered. "When were you going to tell me you could do that?"

"On our twenty-fifth wedding anniversary," she responded, leaning over him and brushing a kiss tenderly across his lips. "Tilly said men get intimidated by women who are stronger than they are until they have more confidence in their relationship."

Cosmos slid his hands up under Terra's arms and rolled suddenly so that she was lying under him. "I think I'll take my chances," he murmured, sealing his lips over hers.

Neither one heard the knock on the door or it slowly opening. Jason poked his head inside and shook his head. He hated breaking the two love birds up but time was short. RITA had informed him a few seconds before that the warehouse was surrounded. Unless they wanted to risk civilians getting hurt, they needed to get their plan moving.

"Uh, Cosmos, I hate to break this up but we need to get our asses in gear," Jason called out. "If you don't leave soon, Avilov will know that even your high-tech jet could never fly that fast. They have to see you leaving, man."

Cosmos slowly finished kissing Terra before he raised his head and gave Jason a quick nod. "Thanks."

"No problem," Jason responded with a respectful nod to Terra who lay flushed and glowing on the tousled bed.

Cosmos reluctantly rose up and held his hand out to help Terra up. He gripped her hand tightly as they walked out of his room. He paused as Terra gently touched her younger brother's arm. Derik looked down at her and smiled sadly before he turned away. Terra glanced once more at Derik before she let Cosmos lead her down the stairwell to the front door.

"I worry about him," she murmured. "Something has happened to him."

"He'll be alright," Cosmos said, noticing the change himself from the excited boy from a few months back that he had first met, to the solemn warrior now. "I'll have a talk with him when this is all over. Maybe he feels like he can't talk about it yet."

"You are a good man, Cosmos Raines," Terra said as he opened the front door and stepped out onto the front step. "Don't you ever forget that."

"I'll just have to get you to remind me when I do," he said huskily. "I'll see you in a few minutes."

"You're damn right you will," she responded, kissing him deeply before stepping back and slowly closing the door behind her.

Cosmos took a deep breath and turned to climb into the taxi that arrived to pick him up. He glanced at the man behind the wheel. He recognized one of Jason's men as the man grinned at him. With a nod, he ignored the feeling of stares causing the hair on the back of his neck to stand up. Jason was going to need Avery's expertise again soon.

* * *

Cosmos watched the video feed on his iPhone. He had sensors all over the adjacent buildings since he realized what was happening. He cursed the fact that he had relied so heavily on the municipal camera system and the ones he had directly hooked to his home base instead of taking a more aggressive stance.

He should have either brought his parents back home or assigned additional security to them. They had several bodyguards, but the men had been killed when they were taken. If he had, his father would be alive today.

Cosmos, you must not blame yourself, Terra's soft voice brushed across his mind. *You did what you could. Now, you must focus on rescuing your mother. If you think of the what-if's, you will leave yourself vulnerable.*

You are a good woman, Terra, Cosmos sent back. *I don't think I've told you that near enough.*

You can show me later, she responded warmly. *I am going through the Gateway now. Come to me, my mate.*

Two more blocks and we should be clear. The jet will take off in fifteen minutes. I have another man who will act as me.

Be safe, she whispered before he felt her mind disconnect as she moved through the Gateway causing his chest to ache at the distance and silence that suddenly swamped him.

Cosmos waited as the driver pulled into a narrow alley. A man stepped out of the back of a building. Cosmos opened the door and nodded to him. They were built almost identically with the same color shaggy brown hair and hazel eyes. Cosmos shrugged out of the coat he was wearing and handed it to the man along with the scarf he had wrapped around his neck. Finally, he handed the man the black leather satchel he was carrying.

"Keep your head down," Cosmos instructed. "We look alike but a facial identification scan will pick up that you aren't me."

The man smiled in amusement. "No one will know. I walk like you, talk like you, and use the same hand gestures. I'll keep my head down and move quickly between the taxi and the jet. I have to get going if this is going to work," he added, slipping the scarf around his neck exactly like Cosmos had worn it.

"Good luck," Cosmos said, turning away.

"I get the easy part," the man said lightly. "I get to travel in style for the next fourteen hours before I get to kick some ass, if you guys leave me any."

Cosmos looked over his shoulder at the man, steely determination glittering in his eyes. "There won't be if I can help it," he said before he pushed the sequence to activate the portable Gateway.

The man and the driver just shook their heads as Cosmos vanished through the shimmering doorway. "I wonder what in the hell his brain looks like under a microscope," the driver muttered under his breath.

"I don't know," Cosmos' double responded with a thoughtful look. "But I bet you it's scary as hell."

Neither man said another word as they got back into the car. There was a lot depending on everyone doing their job. Theirs was to make sure that it looked like Cosmos Raines was getting on a jet for Hong Kong.

Chapter 19

Cosmos nodded to Teriff and the others as he walked into the room set up for their departure. Helene was dressed in a black form-fitting leather outfit that matched the typical Prime Warrior uniform. She had covered her hair with a black knit cap. Brock was scowling as she double-checked the weapons that had been issued to her. Even with her covered from head to toe in the black outfit, there was no denying she was a female. Her long curves easily gave her away.

"Back off!" She snapped as Brock crowded her again.

"You will stay behind me," he demanded angrily.

"Hem!" No! She retorted in Russian. "Not unless it is to shoot your ass so you will get out of my way. Terra, Angus, and I will go after Cosmos' mom while you take out everyone else. If you do your job, then I will not have to worry about getting shot."

"Is everyone ready?" Cosmos asked quietly as his eyes searched the room for Terra.

He breathed a sigh of relief when he saw her thread her way through the warriors. She was dressed the same way as Helene. He was going to have to remember she looked delicious dressed in leather when this was over. His face flushed a little when he felt her soft chuckle in his mind. Pulling his focus back to the task at hand, he looked around the group, pausing when he saw Angus tightening the strap holding his glasses on.

"Angus," Cosmos started to say before the words died in his throat at the narrowed-eyed look the elder Bell gave him.

"I will be with Helene and Terra," Angus said. "Ava knows me. She will need my help and a familiar face."

Cosmos drew in a deep breath, nodding when he realized he would just be wasting precious time and energy trying to change the man's mind. His folks had fallen in love with Angus and Tilly. All four of them were brilliant in their own way.

"Just… keep your head down and follow Helene's orders. Tilly will have my ass if anything happened to you, not to mention Tink, Hannah, and Tansy," Cosmos said grimly.

Borj rubbed his head as he thought of his mate. "Just make sure if it does, Hannah does not have a frying pan near her," he joked to relieve some of the tension.

"Or a hammer," J'kar piped up.

"Or a gun, knife, explosive, throwing star…," Mak said with a grin. "Gods, my Tansy just needs her hands."

"Or a kiss," Angus said with a smile.

The men turned and looked at Angus in puzzlement. "A kiss?" Teriff asked.

Angus' smile turned to a huge grin. "It was a really awesome kiss."

Brawn groaned and rubbed his crotch. "I want to meet some of these females, Teriff. You will be working with my clan as well. Are there females that do not mind a desert environment?"

"Arizona," RITA2 and Angus said at the same time. "Or the Middle East, Africa, parts of Texas…"

"I want a map of your world when we get back," Teriff ordered before he turned. "Right now, though, I want the man who would harm my family," he snarled out, looking at Cosmos as he said it.

"For family," Cosmos replied as RITA2 opened the doorway to an alley not far from the warehouse where his mother was being held in Hong Kong.

* * *

"You each have a comlink with RITA," Cosmos said quietly. "Spread out, but wait for my signal. I'll deploy the sensors. They should be online within thirty minutes. It will take them that long to position and start their feedback to RITA. Once we know whether there is anyone with my mom, and her location, we can start moving in. If the area where she is being kept is clear, RITA will program the position into the Gateway so that Helene, Terra, and Angus can go in and get her out. If not, I'll go in as if I am giving myself up. I'll create a diversion and Helene can take out the target while Angus and Terra get my mom out. You guys are part of that diversion so don't screw this up."

Terra bit her lip, still not liking that part of the plan. "You cannot give yourself up. He will kill you."

Cosmos shook his head as he patted his stomach. "Not with the prototype suit on," he said.

Terra started to protest, but realized that Cosmos was right. Until his mother was safe, they were restricted as to what they could do. The man holding her would use her to force Cosmos to do what he wanted.

"We will wait for your signal," Teriff said and motioned with his hand.

Within seconds, the figures vanished into the darkness. Cosmos pulled the bag he had on his shoulder off and knelt down. Opening it, he pulled out the small box of sensors he had packed.

Opening the box, he accessed the programming for them. "RITA, deploy sensors."

Terra, Angus, and Helene stood back as the tiny silver bugs opened and took off like a swarm of bees heading to their hive. Angus' eyes were wide with awe as he watched the activity. Cosmos fought the small smile that threatened knowing the writer in Angus was already plotting how the sensors would work in his next story. He stuffed the empty box back in the bag and stood.

"Let's go," Cosmos said, looking at the readings coming through his right contact lens. "Helene, I want you, Angus, and Terra to remain at least a block away until we know the location of the guards. If it's clear, RITA will signal for you to do the hop between Baade and the warehouse. If not, be ready to come in, but watch your back. While we will try to engage Avilov's men, he may have a sniper or two that we miss. I've sent the sensors out, but he could have someone placed in an outer building and we might miss them."

"I will," Helene promised quietly. "I will not move until I know it is safe to proceed, and even so, I will still be careful."

Cosmos looked at Terra for a moment before he muttered a low curse. He stepped up to her and pressed a hard kiss to her lips before stepping back again. His eyes glittered fiercely with his struggle between leaving her and wanting to stay.

"Go," she whispered. "I am my father's daughter," she reminded him.

Cosmos nodded and turned, disappearing down the alley. It was time to take out Avilov once and for all. He would not fail his mother.

Chapter 20

"Raines' jet refueled in Hawaii over an hour ago," Afon said. "I have reservations about having him come here."

Avilov looked up with a frown at the current world news he was skimming. Another one of his companies that he thought had been undetectable had been raided. He was down to just a handful now. The current loss would affect his revenues by millions.

"What is it now?" Avilov growled out.

He was getting tired of Afon's continued questioning of his orders. The man was beginning to overstep his boundaries. If he continued, it might be time to start looking for his replacement.

Afon kept his face blank. He was much better at hiding his feelings than the man sitting in front of him. Avilov's face may not be able to show the expression it had before his surgery but his eyes always spoke of what he was feeling. Afon had learned a long time ago when he was just a boy trying to survive to see the next day to look at the eyes.

They always told what a person was planning. He could see his own death in Avilov's eyes. He had already made plans to leave before that happened. He would not kill the man who had taken him off the street and shown him what money and power could do when they were plentiful. He would let Avilov's arrogance be his own downfall.

No, it was time to depart, Afon thought.

He had always trusted his gut feeling. It is what had kept him alive when men like Avilov thought to erase him. He would not be here when Raines arrived. As far as he was concerned, if Raines had one silver-eyed monster working with him then he would have more. He had seen how quickly the male had killed. He was a killing machine. It was time to disappear.

"You have employed me to see to your safety. I have posted additional men around the warehouse should something unexpected arise," Afon said quietly with a bow of his head to show respect. "Is there anything else, sir?"

Avilov stared darkly at his right-hand man's face for several long seconds. Afon made sure he kept his expression blank and his eyes shielded. Avilov rose out of his chair to walk over to the thick, bullet-proof glass he had installed before his arrival. He didn't answer Afon for several minutes as he stared down at where the men were patrolling.

"Have you heard from the team that went into the Raines' warehouse?" He finally asked, turning to stare at the figure standing at attention.

Afon's eyes flickered briefly before he gave a curt nod. "They have taken it and are in the process of photographing and dismantling the equipment," he said stonily, not voicing his doubts about the conversation he had with the man in charge of the mission.

"And the girl?" Avilov pressed with cold, greedy eyes.

"She has been captured," Afon responded. "They will deliver her here per your request."

Avilov grinned in delight. "Good, good. You may go. Send in Frazer," Avilov said, turning and dismissing Afon.

Afon bowed and turned sharply. He knew why Avilov wanted the American mercenary. Afon had been against hiring the man. He was cruel just to be cruel. Afon did not believe in playing with those he killed. It was a good way to get yourself killed if you weren't careful. He believed in killing cleanly and quickly, in and out like a ghost. If you played with your prey, they often turned on you, becoming the predator.

Afon closed the door quietly behind him and headed down the stairs. He called one of the men walking a close perimeter to him and gave the man instructions to have Frazer report to Mr. Avilov's office immediately. Afon straightened the cuff of his pristine dark blue shirt. It was time to leave.

* * *

Cosmos' eyes narrowed as he watched Afon Dolinski step out of the warehouse. He leaned back into the shadows when the man turned and looked in his direction. He knew there was no way the man could see him, but Dolinski didn't move for several long seconds.

He released his breath when he saw the man raise his hand. A moment later, a dark sedan pulled up. A man stepped out of the driver's seat, holding the door open for him. Dolinski made a brief comment to the man before he slid into the driver's seat, shut the door and drove off.

Cosmos frowned as he watched the red tail lights glow briefly as the car slowed to turn the corner. Something was off, but he wasn't sure what it was. Pulling further back, he accessed the sensor information on his contact lens.

Most of them were in place. A few of them were still trying to find a way into some of the rooms in the warehouse. He needed to see if RITA had picked up anything else.

"RITA, full update," Cosmos whispered.

"Teriff and the others are in place. Helene, Angus, and Terra have moved to the top of the building a block away. Avilov's men have expanded their perimeter. There are still four rooms that have not been accessed in the warehouse. You are looking at thirty-eight men. They are heavily armed and wearing protective vests, so aim for head, neck or lower extremity shots. I can take down the security system. They are depending greatly on their manpower. One room is heavily re-enforced with bomb-proof glass and four inch steel re-enforced walls. I'm trying to get a sensor in there now. There is a smaller room off to the right of it. I think your mom may be in there," RITA said. "And Cosmos, be prepared… they have your father's body hanging from the beams," she said as gently as she could. "I'm sorry."

Cosmos leaned back against the brick wall, letting his head fall back as tears burned his eyes at the thought of his father's lifeless body being placed on display. He bit his fist to keep the rage and sorrow from giving him away.

Cosmos, I'm here. Terra's voice caressed his mind. *Do not let him win. Your father cannot hurt any longer. His soul is free and cannot be touched. It is only the shell that remains.*

God, Terra, it hurts so much, Cosmos moaned silently as pain flooded him.

I know, my love. Terra murmured.

Cosmos' eyes glittered and he felt a tear escape at the same time as he swore he could feel her hand caressing his cheek. Warmth flooded him as she poured all of her love into him. He could see images of her holding their child, his mother laughing as a small, dark-haired girl ran up to her, and the four of them strolling along a shoreline covered in pink sand with strange creatures dancing in the surf.

Believe, she whispered softly in his mind.

I do, he responded before he drew in a deep breath to shake off the shock. "RITA, what is the status of Jason's team?"

"It is secure," RITA began, but even Cosmos heard the slight hesitation in her voice.

"Details," he demanded.

"Well... There was a minor issue. It would appear Avilov's men found Runt. Avery isn't happy about that. From what Derik was able to get out of the man they captured, another hacker ratted Runt out for a huge reward. Avilov's men tracked her down through this associate of hers. Bert was injured trying to save her. He'll be alright. He took a bullet to the shoulder.

They were going to use her to hack into me. I let them in because I didn't want the poor girl to get hurt. She was trying everything she could to stop me! Every time I undid the damn lock, she would write a program to seal the door again. I finally had to send her an algorithm to let her know I was aware of what was going on and to let them in. Thank goodness she understood the message I spelled out. Anyway, she fought like a she-devil once the door opened and escaped upstairs. Derik found her hiding under your bed after they took out all but one of Avilov's men. Jason asked Derik to apply some of his persuasive skills and the man sung louder than a canary at a bird seed convention. I was able to replicate his voice and made the call to Dolinski letting him know everything was good. I'm not sure whether or not he believed me from the responses though. He is a very difficult man to read."

"Are you in the last four rooms yet?" Cosmos asked quietly.

"Yes, I'm sending you the information now. I was able to get one of the sensor bugs onto the back of one of the men's jacket as he was entering the re-enforced room. I'm sending a video feed now," RITA said softly. "Your mom is alone in the room to the right. There is a guard stationed outside the door. She appears to be handcuffed to a chair. Her blood pressure is extremely high, Cosmos," RITA warned.

"Send the information to Helene, RITA," Cosmos ordered. "I want mom out of there now."

"Done," RITA said, sending the position of the sensor bug to the portable Gateway. "They are in transport now."

"Let me know the minute she is safe," Cosmos requested.

"I will," RITA responded, monitoring the Gateway.

* * *

Helene heard RITA's soft command in her ear. Turning, she nodded to the two figures standing next to her on the upper landing of a fire escape. They had been forced to hide when a couple of men that were obviously not out for an evening stroll started down the alley they were waiting in. When they encountered another two, the only way had been up if they didn't want to be discovered.

She had to admit, she had been surprised by both of her companions' abilities to silently scale the metal ladder. She waited as Terra opened the shimmering doorway that she was beginning to get used to. A moment later they were in the portal room where Lan was waiting for them. Without waiting, another doorway appeared. The three of them silently slipped through.

Terra's eyes filled with tears as she saw the ravaged expression of hopelessness on the face of the woman chained to the chair in the middle of the semi-dark room. Only a single light shone dimly from a long wire hanging from the ceiling.

She rushed forward, pulling the small tool Mak had given her from her pocket. With a few quick swipes, the laser cut through the thin chain between the thicker wrist cuffs. The woman gasped as her arms fell free to hang limply by her side. She started to slide sideways out of the chair. Angus caught her against his warm body.

"Ava," he whispered quietly in her ear.

"Angus," came the barest hint of a sound as her eyelashes fluttered.

"We're getting you out of here," Angus assured her as he slipped his arm around her and looked at Terra to help him.

"Adam," Ava began before she began to weep softly again.

"I know, sweetheart," Angus whispered. "Cosmos will bring him home."

Ava raised her head in alarm, her eyes pleading with Angus to listen to her. "He mustn't come. That man… he wants to kill my son. I can't let him take them both from me."

"He won't," Terra said, sliding her arm around Ava's other side and helping Angus to stand her up. "My father, brothers, and other warriors are here. They will not let anything happen to him, I promise."

Ava turned her head to stare into Terra's flaming silver eyes. Her soft gasp echoed loudly in the quiet room. Helene turned her head and shook it, frowning.

"We must leave now!" She motioned toward the shimmering doorway.

* * *

"Cosmos, your mom is safe," RITA said. "I'll be there if you need me. Be careful."

Cosmos drew in a steady breath. He knew he was going to need it to deal with what was to come. He wasn't afraid of the fight – he could handle that. It was seeing his father's body and knowing that he would never be able to argue the benefits of video games with him again – or introduce him to the new world he had discovered and the beautiful woman that had captured his heart.

"Teriff, it's a go. The package has been delivered. Time to clean house," Cosmos said, feeling the adrenaline flooding him as rage and the desire for revenge burst over the dam he had built. "I want Avilov alive. To hell with you, Mak, I demand the Right of Justice on that asshole."

"I will be your second," Mak replied quietly. "I've already killed two."

"Damn," Gant muttered. "If this is a contest, I better get my ass in gear."

"Two more down," Hendrik said.

"Eight dead," Teriff added.

Brawn growled. "Show off! I'm going in through the roof."

Cosmos shook his head. He was glad they were on his side. He moved out of the shadows and walked up toward the front of the warehouse. Two men stepped out of the darkened entry way to confront him.

"What do you want?" One of the men asked, spitting on the ground. "This area is closed. Get out of here."

Cosmos stopped in front of the man and smiled. "I have an appointment with your boss. Tell Avilov that Cosmos Raines is here to see him."

The second man started when Cosmos said his name. He touched the mic at his neck and spoke quickly into it. A moment later, he stood back and motioned for Cosmos to walk between them. Cosmos stepped toward the door. A dark smile curved his lips as he watched the number of Avilov's men dropping rapidly on the contact lens in his eye as RITA tracked the number of kills. Cosmos raised his hands out to his side the moment he was between the two men and released a burst of energy out of the palms of his hands from the pads in his gloves. The two men went flying in opposite directions. The count dropped two more points.

Chapter 21

Avilov's face creased into a smile when Frazer informed him that the guards in front had Cosmos Raines. They were bringing him in now. Avilov turned to the man who would replace Afon when this was over.

"Where is Dolinski?" Avilov asked.

Frazer's lip curled in disgust. "He left half an hour ago. He didn't say where he was going, he never does."

Avilov nodded in agreement. That was another reason to get rid of the man. He thought he had the freedom to do what he wanted, when he wanted.

"Kill him when he returns," Avilov said, walking toward the door to his office. "Immediately."

Frazer grinned and stroked the gun at his hip. "With pleasure," he said.

Avilov opened the door and stepped out. He glanced at the man standing guard outside the room next to his before looking down as the door to the warehouse opened.

"Bring her," Avilov ordered the man as he walked by.

He frowned as he walked down the steps. Something was wrong. The only men standing around Raines were the men that had been inside the warehouse. He paused on the steps, forcing Frazer to side-step so he wouldn't run into him. Avilov slid his hand into his pocket, feeling the comfort of the pistol he carried.

"Check him," Avilov ordered.

Frazer stepped around Avilov and jogged down the stairs. There were at least twenty men surrounding him, not counting the guard standing next to the room holding Raines' mother, him, and Frazer. He had another eighteen outside covering the perimeter. There was no way one man could take them all out.

Avilov listened as Frazer demanded that Raines raise his hands above his head. Raines stopped several feet inside the warehouse as if frozen. He stared at the body of his father hanging lifeless from the metal beam supporting a section of the large building for several long moments. Avilov felt a rush of satisfaction knowing the sight of the body would break the billionaire playboy inventor and make it easier to manipulate him. He started to take a step down when those cold hazel eyes swiveled, colliding with his. The smile slowly melted at the look of cold, detached hatred that burned instead of the devastation that he was expecting. Avilov vaguely heard Frazer order Raines to lift his hands again at the same time as the guard behind him murmured that the woman was gone.

As if in slow motion, Raines smiled at him at the same time as he raised his arms. Light flared from his palms, sending two of the men surrounding him flying backwards. Avilov stumbled on the step above him as Frazer shouted out, raising the pistol he held and firing it at Raines. The bullets flashed harmlessly in front of him, lighting up as if they hit an invisible wall before falling harmlessly to the concrete floor. Screams echoed as dark flashes of shadowy figures swept through the warehouse, lifting the men and tossing their broken bodies around as if they were discarded mannequins.

"Kill him," Avilov ordered the guard standing behind him. The man was staring in horror at the massacre below. "Kill him!" He screamed, pushing the man to the side and stumbling up the stairs to his office.

* * *

Cosmos watched as Avilov shoved the man standing on the stairwell behind him to the side. His eyes swiveled back to the man who had ordered him to raise his arms then tried to shoot him when he killed two of the guards. He pulled the laser pistol at his side and aimed it at the man's chest.

Firing once, he struck the man in the center of the chest. The man's eyes widened for a moment before they rolled back in his head. Cosmos switched the charge from stun to kill. He wanted the man alive. He wanted to know who was responsible for his father's death and the man looked like he would be the one to know. Cosmos let Teriff and the others take care of the other men who were firing at anything that moved, including each other.

"Cosmos," RITA said worriedly. "Your suit is getting low. You need to be careful."

Cosmos ignored the warning. His eyes were glued on Avilov who was running down the metal walkway. He strode over to the stairs. The man on the stairwell opened fire on him, emptying one clip and slipping another one in as fast as his trembling fingers would let him. Cosmos calmly climbed up the steps, ignoring the flashes. When the second clip noisily clanged to the stairs, he raised his hand and fired a shot into the man's chest, watching as smoke rose as it penetrated the man's body armor.

"Damn, I guess head or lower extremity shots aren't necessary with that," RITA said in astonishment. "I need to look at the design of your laser pistol again."

Cosmos knocked the body of the man aside, ignoring the sickening thud as it tumbled down the stairs behind him. He continued climbing until he reached the level where Avilov had run. Walking down, he stopped when Teriff's huge frame dropped down in front of him. Blood ran from a cut on his forehead, but otherwise the huge Prime male looked like he had barely broken into a sweat.

"Get out of my way," Cosmos said in an emotionless voice.

Teriff shook his head. "RITA warned me that your suit is depleted. You are defenseless against the weapons without it."

Cosmos ground his teeth in rage. "Get the fuck out of my way, Teriff."

Teriff put his hand on Cosmos' arm, holding him back when he tried to pass him. "Dying will not bring your father back. I will grant you Right of Justice. I will not allow a chance of you being hurt or killed."

Cosmos looked coldly into Teriff's eyes. "I want that bastard," he said hoarsely.

"And you will have him," Teriff responded quietly. "There is a better way of taking him. One that will ensure that none of us are injured or killed. I promised not only my daughter I would not let you come to harm but her mother and Tilly. To tell you the truth, I am much more afraid of them than of you."

"Why?" Cosmos asked, puzzled.

"Let us just say that I took way more cold showers than even RITA2 gave me. Tresa was not very happy with me about sending our daughter off and has not let me forget it yet," Teriff said with a crooked grin.

"The rest are dead," J'kar said, coming up behind his father and impatiently wiping a smear of blood from his arm.

Cosmos turned to look over his shoulder to the ground below. Bodies littered the floor. His gaze moved to where his father's body hung. Empty ropes hung where it had been. He turned startled eyes to Borj who had come to stand next to him.

"Mak has taken your father home to our world," Borj said quietly. "He will be given a warrior's burial."

Cosmos' throat tightened in grief. He nodded before his eyes turned to the closed door. His lips tightened in resolve.

"There was another man," Cosmos said. "I stunned him. I want answers."

"Gant and Brawn have taken him back as well. He will be held for interrogation. You will have the right to decide what is to become of him," Borj stated. "Hendrik, Core, and Bullet will remain here to make sure there are no others. Once we have Avilov, they will return to our world."

"What of Dolinski?" Cosmos asked, looking around with a frown. "He should have been here. I saw him leave earlier."

"We will locate him," Teriff said. "Now, I think it is time to show Avilov what happens when he pisses a Prime Warrior off."

Cosmos nodded solemnly. "And messes with my family."

Chapter 22

Avilov's hands shook as he pulled the drawers out of his desk, tossing them as he searched for additional weapons. He cursed when he only found one additional clip. He looked wildly around, trying to think of how he could escape.

His hand touched his cell phone lying in his jacket pocket. He quickly pulled it out of his pocket and touched the screen. His fingers were shaking so badly that he kept typing in the wrong password. Slamming the phone down on the desk, he held his finger with his other hand as he pressed the numbers. He breathed a sigh of relief when it finally unlocked. He pressed his recent contacts. Seeing Dolinski's name, he pressed the button and picked up the phone, trying to draw in a steadying breath.

On the third ring, Afon Dolinski picked up the call. "Speak," the cold voice said.

"I need you," Avilov said in a trembling voice. "They are all dead. I need you to come get me."

"I no longer work for you, Mr. Avilov," Afon responded coolly. "You are on your own. Goodbye."

Avilov stared at the phone as it disconnected. He frantically pressed at Dolinski's name, but all it did was ring. He dropped the phone onto the desk and backed away. His eyes stared at it blankly for a moment before they jerked up as a shimmering light suddenly appeared in the middle of his office. His hand rose as if in slow motion, but it never got higher than his hip as a burst of light flashed out, striking him in the chest and knocking him backwards against the wall. He raised dazed eyes as Cosmos Raines walked through the doorway followed by four huge shapes. Darkness edged his vision as the largest one pulled him up and slung him over his shoulder. The last thing Avilov saw was the faint outline of his former office before everything went black.

..*

Afon Dolinski looked at the vibrating phone in his hand with a smile. He was free. The man who had held his life in his hands for the past fifteen years was dead or as good as dead. He could feel it. He stood along the edge of the crowded waterway.

Lifting his face to the night breeze, he wondered if he had ever smelled anything so sweet. He looked down at the dark waters and with a strange feeling, as if a weight was lifted from his shoulders, leaned forward and tossed the cell phone into the water. He was a rich man.

It was time to start over - to leave behind everything that had held him captive all of his life. He had done and seen things that most never would. He had been controlled first by his inability to escape the life he was born into, then by the man who had threatened the one thing that had mattered to him. Now, he was in control. Afon Dolinski had died tonight in the shark infested waters of Hong Kong. Aaron Dolan, reclusive billionaire, was suddenly very much alive.

And free, he thought as he turned toward a waiting taxi.

* * *

The first thing Cosmos saw when he walked out of the portal room on Baade was the slender figure standing near the window in the long hallway. He stepped aside so Mak could carry the body of Avilov to the detention cell that he would be held in alongside the other man that was brought back. J'kar followed Mak while Teriff headed in the opposite direction.

Borj came out of the room with a huge, but worried, grin on his face. "I must go," he said with an apologetic slap on Cosmos' shoulder. "Hannah is having pains. Tilly says she had gone into labor. Hannah is threatening to find a 'cast iron' frying pan."

Cosmos nodded absent-mindedly, his eyes never leaving Terra's face. "Congratulations," he murmured.

Borj looked over at Terra, a worried expression on his face. "Will you be there?"

Terra smiled and nodded. "Let mother, Tilly, and Hannah know I will be there shortly."

Borj released a breath of relief before he grimaced and grabbed his stomach. Terra grinned while Cosmos looked on with concern as Borj let out a long groan. Cosmos reached for the huge warrior to steady him when he swayed.

"Borj, what's wrong?" Cosmos asked, holding the man's arm as he drew in a deep breath.

Terra's soft chuckle echoed in the hallway. "I believe Hannah is sharing her labor with him. Tink must have shared the ability to do that with Hannah.

Tink learned during her labor that she could open up and share every aspect of it with J'kar. He complained about the pain so much that I had to give him a sedative. He swore she would never have another child if that was what she had to endure. He said it was worse than any wound he had ever received. This is just the beginning. Hannah will more than likely have many more hours before the babies are born."

"Hours," Borj whispered hoarsely, paling.

"Just remember to breathe," Terra said encouragingly. "You'd better go or she might share the entire experience. Tink finally took sympathy on J'kar and shut him out during the delivery."

"Gods," Borj paled. "I have to go."

Cosmos chuckled as Borj took off at a run down the long corridor. He turned back to stare at Terra who still stood next to the windows. The sun had risen on Baade and she appeared to glow in the early morning light. He walked over to her, opening his arms.

Terra released a soft cry and flew into his opened arms, burying her face in his chest. Cosmos' arms closed around her. It was only then that he realized that both of them were trembling.

I love you, he whispered in her mind. *Thank you for everything.*

I love you so much, Cosmos Raines. You never have to thank me for being there.

"I don't want you to ever think I don't see the things you do for me," he said, pulling back to look down at her. "I want you to know every single day what a beautiful miracle you are to me."

Terra's face softened as she reached up to run her fingers gently down his cheek. "You are silly. Don't you know that I can feel everything that you feel?"

Cosmos gently bit the tips of her fingers when she touched his lips. "I still want to tell you," he said before his eyes darkened. "My mother?"

Terra's own eyes filled with sorrow for Cosmos' mother and her mate. "She is resting. I gave her a sedative. She is hurting. Mak has taken your father's body to be prepared. He will be given a warrior's burial."

Cosmos' eyes filled with tears. He bit his lip and blinked rapidly, looking out the window at the rising sun. A shuddering breath escaped him.

"I thought about what you said," he said quietly. "About him knowing what I was doing. My...," his voice faded as the lump of grief choked him. "The last time I talked to him, my dad said some things that made me think that maybe he knew I wasn't the absent- minded billionaire playboy like the papers and tabloids like to depict me. I'd like to go see my mom."

"I'll take you to her room. I need to go check on Hannah. She wanted to have the babies at her and Borj's home," Terra said, pulling back and squeezing his hand.

Cosmos held her still for a few moments, studying her face intently before he said anything. "When this is over, I want to spend some time with just you."

"Of course," Terra responded lightly with a raised eyebrow. "You do not think I would allow my brothers to be the only ones to experience what labor for a female is like, do you?"

Cosmos chuckled as he let her pull him after her. He knew the next few weeks would be difficult, but he could see the light at the end of the tunnel. His mind was already racing forward. He and Terra would find a way to re-create the mating chemical and as soon as it was perfected, he was going to do everything he could to fulfill the images that Terra had sent him of the happy little girl wrapped in love.

Chapter 23

Two weeks later, Cosmos stood in the center of an indoor arena. It was about the size of a basketball court only with high walls surrounding it. There were only two entrances leading into it. Surrounding the top of the arena stood the figures of the Baade council. The council would observe the challenge, but not interfere. In the top center, Teriff stood looking dark and menacing.

"Cosmos Raines," Teriff's voice echoed over the enclosed room. "You have requested and received permission to administer the Right of Justice against those who have grievously harmed your family. Do you accept that justice will guide your hand and give you the strength to defeat those who have wronged you?"

"I do," Cosmos responded.

Cosmos stood tall as he faced the Prime Leader. A lot had happened over the past two weeks. Cosmos had traveled back and forth between Earth and Baade, meeting with Avery on the cleanup of both his home and the Hong Kong warehouse. Nothing had been found yet of Afon Dolinski.

It was as if the man had disappeared off the face the planet. He was the least of Cosmos' concerns right now. The interrogation of both Avilov and the man named Frazer proved he had the two men most responsible for his father's murder.

He had formally petitioned the council for the Right of Justice. Teriff had immediately accepted his claims. Mak also petitioned and received permission to act as Cosmos' second when he fought against Avilov. Terra had wanted to come, but he had persuaded her to stay with his mother instead. Ava Raines was slowly beginning to wake from the cloud of grief that surrounded her since her husband of thirty years was murdered.

His father had been given a full warrior's burial. It had been a beautiful ceremony held in a sun-filled cavern not far from the city. His father's body was entombed inside the mountain. An inscription of who he was and his life's accomplishments had been carved into the stone.

He and Terra spent hours each day walking with his mother along the shores or through the marketplaces. They showed her the new world she was on and encouraged her to talk about her grief when she felt like it. Terra and Tresa's gentle touch, as well as Tilly's exuberance and determination to provide sex education to the Prime males and females, slowly brought small smiles to his mother's face once again. Angus was always there to support his mom when she would droop. He never said much, just provided the strong arm that she needed when Cosmos wasn't with her.

Cosmos' last return to Earth brought additional good news, Merrick had been found alive. Rose and Trudy had narrowed the search to a small clinic outside of Reno, Nevada thanks to an anonymous caller. Avery, her crew, and several special agents sent in by the President, staged an operation and were able to get him out. They had their hands full when he promptly took off on a wild chase after the female who had alerted them to his location. Merrick promised Avery he would return to the warehouse as soon as he caught the female who had worked at the facility where he had been held.

Now the only ones he was worried about were Garrett and Rico. Both men were still missing. Each of the Clan Leaders promised they would search their regions for the two missing men and the female that had been with them. There had been no word on the other female they had been trying to rescue. The skimmer carrying her had not been located yet and because the warriors who had attacked the fortress had dismantled the emergency tracking device, there was no way to electronically locate it.

Cosmos focused back to the task at hand when Teriff slammed the gavel down in front of him. He turned as a door slid open on the opposite side of the arena. Two guards pushed Frazer out of the opening. One of the guards released the restraints around his wrists before stepping back through the opening and closing the door again.

Teriff glared down at the other human male. "Human, you have been accused of causing grievous harm to this man and his family. You have admitted to killing his father. He has demanded the Right of Justice and he has been granted the right to avenge this wrong."

Frazer spit onto the dirt floor, then wiped the dirty sleeve of his shirt across his mouth. Hatred burned in his eyes. He had learned the hard way that the Prime's idea of interrogation was to almost kill him over and over until he told them what they wanted to know. Just when he thought he would finally find relief from the pain, they would heal him and do it all over again until he thought he would go mad. The problem was they wouldn't let him. They fucking healed his shattered mind, not even giving him the relief of insanity.

"Right of Justice," he sneered, looking at where Cosmos stood. "What justice is there when he gets to kill a defenseless man?"

Teriff looked down at Frazer in disgust. "As the accused, you are allowed to choose one of the weapons against the wall to defend yourself with. Which do you choose?"

Frazer looked over to the side and saw three weapons attached to the wall on his side of the arena. He glanced at all the men watching him before turning to walk over to the rack. There was a long knife, a spear with a sharp blade at the tip, and a broad sword.

He immediately discarded the sword. It would be heavy and he would tire easily. The spear had possibilities. The blade on the end had one smooth edge and one jagged edge. He could slice with it or saw through the bastard. His eyes flickered to the knife.

He was damn good with a knife, but that meant close range combat. His eyes glanced back to where Raines stood stiffly, watching him. His eyes moved back to the weapons and his hand wavered back and forth between the knife and the spear. At the last minute, he grabbed the spear.

This shouldn't take long with pretty boy and I can always use the knife if I have to fight again, Frazer thought with a menacing grin as he turned back to face Raines.

"I choose the spear," Frazer called out. "If I win, what happens next?"

Teriff's face remained carved in stone. "You will go free," he replied. "Only Cosmos has asked for the Right of Justice against you. Your friend has not been so fortunate. Two requests have been granted against him."

Frazer spit on the ground again and grinned up at Teriff. "Avilov's no friend of mine," he replied. "I want passage back to my world once this is over."

Teriff sneered. "Granted. I don't want your stench on my planet," he responded coldly before turning to Cosmos. "The weapon of justice is the spear. You will face off inside the center circle and wait until I give the command to start. Once you begin, the doors to the arena will be opened only when one of you remains alive."

Cosmos bowed his head in respect. He turned to walk over to the weapons on his side of the arena. He had only taken a few steps when Mak's roar of rage warned him that Frazer was not going to wait for him to get his weapon or enter the circle. Cosmos ducked and twisted as the sharp blade danced across the area he had been standing. The smooth blade sliced a thin, shallow cut across his upper shoulder as he grabbed Frazer's other arm and shoved him away.

"You bastard," Cosmos growled out as Frazer twisted around to face him. "Even given an opportunity to win your freedom in a fair fight, you would cheat."

Frazer smiled as he circled around Cosmos. He jabbed the spear toward him, deftly putting his body between Cosmos and his weapons. He charged toward Cosmos again.

Instead of turning away like Frazer expected, Cosmos twisted just enough that the long shaft slid between his arm and his body. Cosmos grabbed the shaft with both hands and brought his knee up, catching Frazer in the stomach at the same time as he twisted the spear. The move caught Frazer by surprise, allowing Cosmos to jerk the spear out of the slightly larger man's hands.

Cosmos stepped back with the spear in his hands as Frazer went down on one knee, gasping for breath. He held one hand to his stomach while the other touched the dirt ground in an effort to support himself. Frazer warily rose, never taking his eyes off where Cosmos stood confidently swirling the spear between his hands before he brought it down against his side and struck a pose that spoke of his skill as a fighter.

Fear raced through Frazer as he realized that he had made a very serious mistake. He had underestimated Raines. He had believed all the newspaper and tabloid reports about him being nothing more than a playboy billionaire who spent his time either in his lab, or with the ladies. The confidence of his stance and the look in his eyes spoke of a man who not only knew how to fight but how to win.

"Get your weapon," Cosmos growled. "When you die, you will do so knowing what it feels like to be totally helpless."

* * *

Frazer backed up toward the rack of weapons on Cosmos' side of the arena. He turned briefly, glancing over his shoulder at where Cosmos stood watching him. He reached out both hands, grabbing the spear off the rack. As he turned, his other hand slipped down and pulled the knife off as well. He slipped it into the back waistband of his pants.

Turning around until he was facing the man waiting patiently for him, he twirled the spear between his hands as well. He had no intentions of dying. If killing Raines was his way off this damn world, he didn't have a problem doing it. He had been looking forward to killing him anyway; now there was just more incentive.

Walking toward the circle, he stepped inside it and struck a fighting stance. He waited as Raines walked toward the circle. He was wary now as he picked up clues about the man walking toward him. He noticed the way Raines walked on silent feet with an easy, relaxed gait. His fingers held the spear in a light but firm grip. Raines' eyes stayed focused on him, not on his weapon like someone who was new to fighting would do. Sweat beaded as he realized that getting out of this alive wasn't going to be as easy as he thought it would be.

"Let's do this," Frazer snapped out as his apprehension built.

Cosmos' lips curled in a cold sneer. "Now, we fight," he said as he stepped into the circle and positioned himself.

Chapter 24

Cosmos knew the moment Frazer realized not only his mistake, but that he was not going to be as easy to defeat as the man first thought. Frazer was over-confident in his ability to bully his opponents. He used his strength and intimidation to try to overwhelm them. Cosmos struck out quickly with the tip of the spear the moment Teriff called out to begin. He sliced a deep cut over Frazer's shoulder in the same exact place as Frazer had cut him.

Frazer's grunt of pain pulled a mocking chuckle from Cosmos. He planned on drawing a lot of those grunts before he killed the bastard. He pulled on the cold rage burning inside him. He let the image of his father's body hanging limply from the beam in the warehouse and the pale face of his mother give him the cold focus he needed to defeat the man in front of him.

Cosmos parried the shaft as Frazer moved in a small circle around him, knocking it casually to the side. He returned it with a clean slice to the backside of Frazer's left calf. The curse from the man echoed in the quiet arena. The only sound was the slight scuffle of their feet in the dirt and Frazer's heavy breathing.

"I'm going to kill you pretty boy," Frazer taunted. "Did I tell you how your father begged me to let them go right before I shot him? How he whined about not knowing anything about your inventions?" He sneered, slicing through the air at Cosmos' neck.

Cosmos bent backwards, the blade missing his neck by scant millimeters. He twisted and sliced a long cut across Frazer's stomach.

"Go on," Cosmos said quietly, not showing any emotion.

Frazer snarled when he didn't get the response he was expecting and jabbed the spear at Cosmos' stomach. He followed by kicking out with his leg, striking a glancing blow to Cosmos' side. He grunted when Cosmos returned the blow by twisting low and knocking his feet out from under him with the spear. Fear glazed his eyes before fury poured through him when Cosmos drew two matching cuts along each of his cheeks from just below his eye to his jaw.

He rolled and scrambled to his feet as Cosmos stepped back. He pressed the sleeve of his shirt against the burning sting of the cut on his right cheek. The sleeve came away smeared in blood. Hatred burned like fire in the pit of his stomach. He knew that Raines was just toying with him.

"Why the fuck don't you just kill me?" Frazer said harshly.

Cosmos swirled the spear in front of him and motioned with his fingers for Frazer to attack. A dark smile curved his lips as he took in the blood from the cuts he had made. There would be many more, each slowly draining the man of strength until he felt weak and helpless.

"I will," Cosmos promised, remaining poised.

Over the next two hours, Cosmos drew more and more cuts across Frazer until the man staggered as he tried to remain standing. The last slice had cut him diagonally across the chest from one side to the other. Cosmos watched as the spear fell from Frazer's hands and he sank to his knees.

"Kill me," Frazer said hoarsely.

"Stand up," Cosmos responded coldly, wiping the blood out of his left eye where the tip of Frazer's spear had opened a small cut right above it.

Frazer's head dropped down until his chin rested on his chest. His hands fell limply to his side. He looked defeated but Cosmos wasn't about to believe that a man like Frazer would just accept death, not when he still could draw a breath.

Cosmos patiently waited until Frazer's head rose. The cold, calculating look of hatred shown clear, proving what he thought - Frazer would not give up as long as he lived. His eyes flickered briefly to the spear that was lying just out of reach of the man kneeling in front of him. His eyes jerked up in time to see the slight movement of Frazer's hand as he reached behind him.

Pain exploded through Cosmos as he realized that Frazer had taken not one but two weapons. He staggered as the long blade of the knife embedded to the hilt in his right thigh. He fell backwards onto the ground as the loud roars of rage echoed from those watching around the arena. His eyes turned to Teriff and J'kar who were holding Mak back. A soft cry sounded faintly before it was concealed.

Terra! Cosmos painfully bit out.

He is getting up! Cosmos, he has his spear. No one can help you. The council will only let Mak finish him for fighting with dishonor if you are killed, Terra cried out.

Cosmos pushed Terra's voice and his pain to the back of his mind. He gripped his spear tightly in his left hand while he wrapped his right hand around the hilt of the knife. He watched through a haze of pain as Frazer staggered over towards him. Hatred and triumph gleamed in his eyes.

"You should have killed me while you had the chance, Raines," Frazer gloated. "Now your mommy can cry over your grave too."

Cosmos waited until Frazer stopped just in front of him. When the man raised his arm to drive his spear into him, Cosmos lunged forward, driving his own spear through the stomach of the man who had murdered his father while ripping the knife from his thigh and driving it through the man's throat. A roar of pain ripped from his lips as the blade pulled from his flesh.

Frazer's eyes widened in surprise, his hands opening in reflex as the two blades pierced him before glazing over and becoming empty. Cosmos fell backwards into the dirt, thrusting Frazer as far away from him as he could before he collapsed.

"Cosmos!" Terra's cry echoed around him.

Things began to blur as he stared up at the ceiling of the arena. His mind processed the fact that he had been so focused on killing Frazer that he had not even bothered looking up at the ceiling. It was a truly beautiful piece of artwork. Intricate murals depicting different warriors battling covered the arched surface. The colors were bold and the more he stared the more he saw. At times, he could swear they actually moved. He blinked rapidly when they went out of focus. He wanted to study them and wondered vaguely if his fight with Frazer would ever be depicted up there. Maybe after he was dead, they would paint it.

You will not die, Terra admonished him as she gently lifted his head.

Why do I feel so tired? Cosmos asked with a frown. *Did he hit an artery?*

I think you nicked it when you pulled the knife out of your leg, she said in reproach. *Didn't you think a spear through his heart enough?*

I didn't get his heart, Cosmos said, feeling his eyes drooping even though he tried to keep them open. *I went through his stomach. The acid alone would be devastating to the organs surrounding it.*

Hush now, you silly man, and let me take care of you, Terra murmured as she spoke softly to someone else standing near her.

I want to have a baby, Cosmos muttered suddenly.

Soft laughter filled his mind. *Let me keep you alive first, then we will talk about having a baby.*

Avilov? Cosmos whispered faintly.

Mak is excited that he will have a chance to kill someone. He is really very upset that the man touched his mate. I think he would have knocked you out anyway, so he could have his chance at him, Terra responded lightly.

Cosmos smiled as he thought of Avilov facing the huge Prime warrior without his lackeys to protect him.

He felt a tug on his leg and heard the sound of material ripping but everything seemed to be coming from a great distance. His mind tried to analyze and record everything but it was getting hard to remain focused. A soft brush of warmth washed over him, pulling at him as if there was suddenly someone tightly holding on to him.

I've got you, Terra whispered as everything faded around him. *Rest, my love.*

Chapter 25

Cosmos had to blink several times before things started to come back into focus. His head felt like it was full of cotton and his body felt like lead. He shifted his right hand under the soft material of the bedspread covering him, sliding it down to his thigh where the knife had struck him. He was surprised to feel only a slightly raised line of skin. The area around the line was a little tender but nothing like it should have been.

"You will always have a faint reminder, but once the hair grows back over it, you will not even be able to see it," Terra's soft voice said from beside the bed.

Cosmos turned his head. He couldn't see her face. It was cast in shadows with the sun streaming through the window behind her. He knew he was in their living quarters at the palace. He looked back around as the sound of a throat clearing in the doorway drew his attention away from her. Teriff stood at the entrance, watching him.

"Hey," Cosmos said weakly.

Teriff raised his eyebrow. "I am not sure what that means but I will assume that you will live," Teriff said dryly, stepping into the room.

"Of course he will live," Terra snapped sternly as she rose from the chair she had been sitting in and crossed over to sit on the edge of the bed. "He was never in any danger. I was protecting his life force with my own."

Teriff's eyes darkened as he remembered how close he came to losing his beautiful daughter and the mate he had come to respect as a son. He pulled a chair that was by the door closer to the bed and sat down heavily. He studied his daughter and her mate for several moments before he cleared his throat.

"I wanted to tell you I was wrong about you," Teriff began gruffly, looking with a solemn expression at Cosmos. "I'm... sorry."

Cosmos' eyes widened at the huge warrior's words. "Hold on, I need to be sitting up to hear this," he muttered as he struggled to sit upright.

He nodded his thanks when Terra helped him. He leaned forward so she could stack the pillows behind him. Leaning back against them, he grabbed her hand when she made to move away again. There was no way he was letting her get away from him, not after he thought he had lost her for a minute or two there in the arena. He pulled her down against him on the bed, tucking her firmly under his arm.

"Okay, can you repeat that?" He asked with a small grin.

Teriff released a loud sigh. "Tilly and Tresa both said you would enjoy this. I won't even start to tell you what RITA2 said," he muttered.

"I told him he better be prepared to eat a lot of crow," RITA2 responded, shimmering into a solid form in the middle of the room.

"Holy shit!" Cosmos muttered, his jaw dropping as he saw a fully corporeal figure materialize. "How the hell were you able to do that? I mean, I know you had a holographic shape down, but this is... this is incredible!"

RITA2 giggled and winked. "DAR, darling, I need you!" RITA2 called out in a husky voice filled with amusement.

A moment later, the dark form of a massive Prime warrior appeared next to her. The sculptured face and form was even larger than Mak who was considered unusually large for a Prime male. What drew Cosmos' attention the most were the dark silver eyes that burned with an unnatural light.

"You called, my love?" DAR replied in a deep voice.

RITA2 winked and grinned. "I programmed him to say that," she whispered dramatically.

"Not likely," DAR replied dryly. "If you remember, I was the one who wrote the script that allowed the programming to create this form."

RITA2 giggled as he slid his arm around her curvy figure. "We are working with RITA to get her a shape. We already have FRED and she is just dying to develop the script for what she is going to look like. She has already talked to Tilly about if she would mind using Lucy's form," RITA2 said, referring to Tilly's grandmother who had been a member of the French Underground during World War II.

Cosmos snapped his jaw shut, wondering what in the hell he and Tilly had done. Their programming was taking on a life of its own. He could already see the possibilities and the problems that could develop.

RITA2 stepped closer to the bed, leaning over to brush a kiss across Cosmos' forehead. He could almost imagine feeling soft lips touching his skin. She stood back and wrapped her arm around DAR with a small sigh.

"You know," she said quietly. "I've always thought of you more as my son than as my creator or a father figure. I'm glad you are okay, Cosmos, and very sorry RITA and I couldn't have done something to save your father."

Cosmos stared at the curvy redhead standing in front of him. If it wasn't for the fact he knew she wasn't a real form, he would never have guessed that she wasn't human. Warmth flooded him as feelings rushed through him as he realized that she looked just like he always imagined she would if she was human.

"Thanks, RITA2," Cosmos responded. "I like your new form – as a friend," he hastily added when DAR shot a dark, glowing look at him.

RITA2's laughter echoed as she began to fade. "Come on, darling. I wanted to show you a new replication script I was thinking about."

"Replication program?" Teriff said, looking at Terra and Cosmos in horror.

"Oh God," Cosmos said with a laugh. "I hope she wasn't referring to what I think she was!" His mind filled with images of little RITAs and DARs running through the palace.

Teriff's eyes narrowed for a moment before he stood up with a nod. "You are alive. I have said I am sorry. Now I want more grandbabies. I will leave you to work on it. I expect them soon. I must go now. Tink and J'kar are bringing their daughters to me so I may watch them. I have promised them a 'horsey' ride," he said proudly before he turned to leave. He paused at the door, looking at Cosmos once more. "You are a worthy warrior. I know you will protect my daughter well," he added before he gave one more brisk nod and left them alone.

* * *

Cosmos watched as Teriff left. They heard the outer door close before Cosmos tilted his head back and rested his head against the headboard. He wondered how long he had been out of it for so much to happen.

Three days, Terra replied, resting her cheek against his bare chest. *There was more damage to the artery than I first realized and you bled heavily.*

Avilov? Cosmos asked, enjoying talking to Terra this way. It felt more intimate. *What happened to him?*

Mak was very happy to stand in as your second as he had already been granted, Terra responded. *The council agreed as Frazer fought without honor and Mak had a sound case against Avilov to allow him to go ahead and fight the male. I was not there for the fight but from what I heard, it did not take as long for Mak to kill him as my brother had hoped. The man fought, but he was not a warrior. RITA2 said my brother toyed with him as long as he could before Avilov collapsed from blood loss and died. The healer who pronounced his death said the man already had damage to his heart and would not have survived much longer anyway.*

You were not supposed to be there for my fight with Frazer. You were supposed to stay with my mother, Tilly, and your mom, Cosmos gently admonished, running his hand up and down her arm as she shivered.

They wanted me to go to you, including your mother, Terra replied huskily. *It's a good thing that I did. You would have died if I had not wrapped your life force with my own.*

Cosmos didn't reply as Terra showed him everything that happened through her memories. Vivid images filled his mind as she relived his fight with Frazer. Her fear and horror rolled through him as he saw Frazer throwing the knife he had taken. As if watching a movie, he saw an image of himself strike out at Frazer when the man moved to kill him. He saw the knife being ripped from his leg and the blood pooling around him as it cut into the main artery in his thigh. He would have been dead in minutes from blood loss if not for Terra.

"I love you," he said huskily, pulling her tighter against him. "Thank you… for everything."

Terra looked up at him. "I was so scared I would lose you," she whispered in a choked voice. "I never want to see you covered in blood like that again. I could feel you dying and I felt so helpless because they would not let me go to you until Frazer was declared dead."

Cosmos leaned down, brushing a kiss across her mouth. The soft tremble of her lips drew a loud groan from him. His body tightened. Three days of sleep and restorative healing suddenly reset his body back to the normal buzz that powered him.

"If you are my nurse, I think I might need help with my bath," Cosmos murmured against her lips with a wicked twinkle glittering in his eyes. "I would hate to have a relapse or anything."

Terra blushed as she saw the tented cover of the sheet over his lap. She pulled back and smiled seductively as she slid out of the bed. Reaching down, she jerked her shirt over her head, revealing she wasn't wearing anything under it.

Cosmos drew in a sharp breath as his eyes soaked in the smooth heavy globes and dark centers. "Damn! I think I'm going to be under your tender care for a long, long time," he hissed, scrambling out from under the covers of the bed.

Terra hurried around when he swayed for a moment. "Are you sure you are up to this?" She asked anxiously as she slid her arm around his waist.

"Oh yeah," he said with a grin, looking down, not at her but further.

Terra's eyes followed his and she gasped as she saw his cock jerking up and down. The long, thick bulbous head swelled even more as she gazed down at it. Cosmos' chuckle drew her attention back up to his face.

"If you keep staring at me like that, I don't think I'm going to make it to the bathroom," he murmured, sliding his arm up until he was cupping her left breast in the palm of his hand. "I told you I wanted a baby. I meant it," he said softly, looking deeply into her eyes.

Terra smiled up at him before she guided him to their bathing room. "Well, you heard my father. He wants more grandbabies. I think we should start working on it. According to Tilly, the more you practice, the better you get."

Cosmos groaned as he felt her brush the tip of his cock with her hand as she stepped over the lip of the sunken tub. *Hell, if she gets any better I'll die of pleasure,* Cosmos thought as she pulled him down into the swirling warm water.

* * *

Cosmos leaned back against the edge of the huge tub. It was more than big enough for the two of them. He closed his eyes as he felt Terra's strong fingers begin to massage the soap into his skin. He wanted to savor the feel of her touching him. Never had he ever experienced the feelings he did with her. He didn't know if he would ever be able to tell or show her just how much she meant to him but he would spend the rest of his life trying.

A low moan escaped him as she straddled him and carefully poured warm water over his head. She gently wiped the water from his face with a soft cloth before he heard her pour some shampoo into her hand. A moment later, he felt her fingers as they scraped lightly over his scalp. She rose up and down as she worked the shampoo from front to back. Unable to help himself, he cracked his eyelids open just enough to watch her.

Cosmos gulped as his eyes met the dark rosy areolas and taut nipples of her breasts as she rose up again. He could feel his breathing increase and his mouth water as she leaned forward and worked her fingers through his hair that had grown a little longer over the past couple of months.

When her left nipple brushed his lips, he opened his mouth and latched onto it – sucking hungrily. Her hands fisted in his hair, tugging just enough to add a little pain with the pleasure. Her short gasping breaths echoed loudly.

"Cosmos," she panted. "Oh yes, baby."

Cosmos released her nipple with a pop and leaned back. "I like it when you call me that," he said with a twinkle.

"I like it when you suck on my breasts," Terra admitted. "It 'turns me on' as Tilly would say."

Cosmos grimaced. "I'm not sure I want to know what else Tilly has been teaching you," he said with a look of disgust on his face.

"I don't know," Terra teased. "I've found the information to be very enlightening and some of it is downright fascinating. How about I just show you instead?" She suggested, lowering her head to seal her lips against his as she began rotating her hips. "I'll start with the lap dance," she breathed out.

"Oh... hell," Cosmos whispered hoarsely as his head fell back in pleasure.

Chapter 26

Cosmos shuddered as Terra rotated, swiveled, and rocked her hips and upper torso. At the same time, she continued washing and rinsing his hair. The combination of the slippery soap, her soft flesh, and her fingers fleetingly touching him everywhere was enough to drive him crazy.

His cock was as hard as a steel pipe and throbbing in time with her touch. Every time he would reach for her, she would stop and shake her head. She murmured something about Tilly saying foreplay led to more satisfaction during love-making. Cosmos didn't give a damn about foreplay right now. As far as he was concerned, she had moved from foreplay to torture the moment she straddled him.

He drew in swift breaths as her hands moved over his chest, tangling in the light hair covering it and gently pulling on it. He cried out when she teased his nipples with her lips, tongue, and teeth. His eyes followed the line of her spine as she sank further into the water and lifted her ass up just enough that the water teased him with hints of silky flesh.

"Terra… baby," Cosmos mumbled as she wrapped her hand around his throbbing length. "Please baby, enough foreplay."

She leaned forward and brushed a kiss across his lips before drawing his bottom lip between her teeth. "Not yet," she whispered, letting his straining member go and moving her hand down between his legs. "I'm not finished washing you."

"Oh God," he groaned, lifting his hips up as her hands slid around to his ass. "You're going to kill me."

Her hands stilled for a moment. Cosmos forced his eyes open to see why she froze. Her worried eyes stared at him for a moment before a smile of understanding crossed her face. She had thought he meant it literally.

"With pleasure, baby," he assured her. "I'm loving what you are doing," he whispered. "Just don't tell Tilly… please."

"She pointed out some spots that were very sensitive and known to heighten the pleasure for a male," Terra said reassuringly. "I want to give you a lot of pleasure."

Cosmos bit back a curse as she scraped her nails lightly over his taut buttocks, running them up to where his ass and spine met. She continued to rub the area, drawing long moans of pleasure from him before moving down his legs where she paused when she reached his ankles. There she massaged the dip between his heel and ankle bone. A shuddering moan escaped him as she hit the pressure point there.

"Wait until I do that when I am on top of you and you are buried deep inside me," Terra whispered. "It is supposed to drive a man wild."

Cosmos' eyes popped open as the last of his control snapped. It was about time to show Terra that she and Tilly weren't the only two well versed in the art of torture when it came to pleasuring. With a growl, he reached down and rolled until Terra was under him.

"My turn to wash!" He growled out.

Terra's eyes widened at the rough edge to his voice. Tilly had warned her that things could get very exciting if the male reached his breaking point. Terra had questioned Tilly on what she meant, but the older woman just gave her a secretive smile and a word of advice.

"Just hang on and enjoy the ride, honey," Tilly had advised with a dreamy look in her eyes. "It is better than any roller coaster."

Terra trembled as Cosmos' calloused palms slid over her skin. The slight roughness of his hands arousing her already heated flesh to a new level. He poured soap into his palms and rubbed them together. A dark smile creased his face as he wrapped his hands around her neck. The slight pressure of his thumbs as they stroked her with delicate little circles heightened the sense of vulnerability his voice had awakened. Her body didn't react like it was in danger of being hurt, more like the danger of being out of control.

"Cosmos," Terra whispered with a hint of uncertainty.

"Trust me," he murmured as he kissed her deeply.

Cosmos felt her open to him. Her tongue moving tentatively to touch his before the fire exploded inside her as his hands moved lower. A part of him wanted to claim her, possess her, and mark her so that every male that saw her would know that she belonged to him. But, there was another part of him that burned even brighter with a different desire. He wanted to touch, explore, and cherish her so that there wasn't a part of her he did not know. He felt torn as the two desires raged inside of him. The first scaring him as he had never felt that way about any female before and the second terrifying him even more because he knew she would know him just as well.

Both, Terra moaned as his fingers slid deep inside her. *I choose both parts.*

Good choice, Cosmos groaned back as he pulled back far enough to flip her over so she was facing away from him. *Grip the edge of the tub.*

* * *

Terra grasped the side of the tub. Her fingers curled on the slippery side as she clung in desperation as Cosmos continued to wash her body. His touch was everywhere, leaving no part of her body unexplored. Her breath exploded out of her as his hands ran over her breasts, down over her flat stomach, to the vulnerable flesh of her folds. His fingers touched, caressed, and explored as they moved in and out of her hot channel leaving her quivering for more.

"Please," she begged as he pulled his fingers back across the triangle nubs that formed her clitoris.

"Foreplay, baby," Cosmos said as he kissed the back of her neck. "Just relax and enjoy," he whispered.

Cosmos ran tiny kisses against the back of her neck as he ran his left hand over the three swollen nubs between her legs. When she arched back against him, he slipped his right hand down along the crack of her ass before slipping two of his fingers into the tight ring.

He continued kissing her while pumping in and out of her and rubbing at the same. The combined sensations were too much for Terra. Her hoarse scream echoed through the room as she melted in his arms as her first orgasm exploded from her. He didn't stop until her head drooped against his arm, her body shaking with reaction.

She moaned softly as he pulled his fingers out of her. He smiled as he felt her silent protest at the feeling of emptiness. He stood up, sweeping her limp, wet body into his arms. He was done with the foreplay. He was ready to get to the love-making.

Terra's drowsy eyes opened. "There is more?" She whispered, dazed.

Cosmos chuckled as he set her down so she was leaning against the counter. He reached for a towel and began drying her off. His hands trembled slightly as he knelt in front of her to carefully dry her legs. He knew that the trembling had nothing to do with his recent injury and everything to do with the overwhelming love he had for the woman standing before him.

He looked up when he felt her touch his brow. "I love you, my mate. Never doubt that," she said, looking at him with her heart exposed.

Cosmos smiled and tenderly finished drying her. When he was done, he quickly ran the towel over his own body before he swept her up into his arms again. He focused on making it to the bed. His body was taut with need. He knew he wouldn't last long, but was determined that she would come once more, with him.

Setting her down on the bed, he ran his hands over her shoulders pushing her back until he lay over her. His mouth hungrily devoured hers. His lips becoming more frantic as his desire threatened to break the control he fought to retain. Terra moved restlessly under him, arching and rolling her hips as she answered the call of her mate.

"Now," Cosmos growled out as her legs wound around his waist. He pushed forward, impaling her on his throbbing cock. "Now!" He groaned, pumping into her slick heat.

"Cosmos," Terra moaned.

She gripped his shoulders as he pushed into her hard enough to push her upward. Her heels dug into his ass, clinging to him as he moved faster. The friction of his cock against her swollen clitorises and vagina was too much after the intense orgasm she'd had just minutes before. Her body clenched around his as another orgasm burst from her. As her body fisted his, Cosmos muttered a loud curse as his body reacted. His balls drew up tight and he felt the tingling right before he thrust once more, spilling his seed deep into her womb. A long, loud moan escaped him as he froze above her. Terra could see the muscles in his neck and shoulders strain and the fierce, tight look on his face as he came. His body shuddered violently before he collapsed over her.

His face dropped down until it was hidden in the curve of her neck. He pulled her close even as his body continued to shudder from the aftermath of his orgasm. Nothing had prepared him for such a release. He murmured softly against her skin when she pulled her legs down from around his waist.

"What?" She asked rubbing her hand tenderly along his back.

Cosmos pulled his head up and looked down at her with shining eyes. "I said, we are one," he whispered. "I love you, Terra. Forever."

"I love you too, my warrior," she murmured drowsily.

Cosmos gently pulled out of her and rolled to his side, drawing her back into his arms. He knew she was exhausted from caring for him. He rubbed her back tenderly until he felt her fall into a deeper sleep. His own eyes grew heavy as his body relaxed, sated from their love-making.

Together we'll find the solution to the mating chemical, he thought. *Together we'll make having a baby possible.*

Chapter 27

Cosmos sank back down into the soft grass, watching as his mother and Terra picked flowers to go on the table for dinner. They were visiting with her, Tilly, and Angus at Mak's mountain home. Mak had pretty much turned the house over to Tilly, Angus, and his mother since Tansy preferred living on the island home he had not far from Hannah.

He turned his head to stare up at the clouds as they drifted by, feeling happy and content. Tink and J'kar's twin daughters, Wendy and Tessa, were a handful just like their mother. They were into everything. Hannah's twins, a girl named Ocean and a boy named Sky, were not far behind.

Cosmos couldn't help but grin at the mischief the four toddlers had gotten into when they visited them a month ago. They had taken a shine to coloring the wall in Teriff's office with the crayons Tilly had brought back with her one afternoon when he was watching them. Teriff refused to let Tink and Hannah clean it off, saying he would treasure their artwork as if it was a Masterpiece. Since Tansy and Mak's twins, Sonya and Mackenzie, were born, Teriff had been pestering him and Terra about when they were going to add to his list of 'Grandkids' so he could be a really great 'Grand' father.

He sat up and looked over to where his mother and Terra were when he heard a deep voice call out his mom's name. A smile pulled at his lips when he saw her blushing as Lal, one of Teriff's guards, walked toward her. She straightened, pulling her shoulders back. She had a slightly defiant expression on her face as she watched the huge, older warrior approach her.

It had been almost a year since his fight in the arena and life was almost as full as the vision Terra had sent to him that day long ago. While there was not a little girl running, giggling toward his mom, there would be soon.

They had spent months analyzing the chemicals from Terra's brothers. Her brothers had happily gathered samples as it meant they got to have sex often on the pretense, not that they needed any, of helping out Cosmos and their sister's research. Terra discovered a chemical in the saliva that produced a reaction in the female, causing her body to release the eggs her body stored and softening the lining of her uterus.

Once they were able to duplicate the chemical, Terra was given an injection. After a few changes in the dosage, she became pregnant. Before long, news of their research reached other couples who were trying unsuccessfully to have children. Terra ended up opening a clinic one week a month so she could meet with the couples. Her research now focused almost exclusively on reproductive issues for her people.

Cosmos smiled as he watched Terra's rounded form straighten as she called out a greeting to Lal. His eyes softened as he studied her. She glowed with happiness. He watched as she talked for a moment with the older warrior before excusing herself. He smiled when she turned toward him and winked as she walked through the ankle-length grass. She sank down next to him, leaning forward to give him a soft kiss.

He pulled her into his arms and lay back on the grass again, being careful of her rounded belly. He rested his hand on the soft swell and grinned when he felt the movement under it. He shifted so she could lay with her stomach resting on him.

"Lal is determined to woo your mother," Terra murmured. "Tilly has been working on both of them."

"I saw the mating mark on her hand, even though she tried to hide it," Cosmos said. "I think she is worried not enough time has passed since dad died."

Terra leaned up over him and rested her hand against his cheek. She looked down into his beautiful hazel eyes. She could still feel his pain when he thought of his father.

"Do you think your father would be upset about Lal and her?" She asked curiously.

Cosmos shook his head. "No, he would be happy for her. He wouldn't want her to be alone any more than she would want him to be," he said, turning his head to see where Lal was bending to pick up a flower that his mother dropped. "She won't have any choice, anyway. They were meant to be together. The mating mark isn't something to be ignored or denied. I know because I tried at first."

Terra laughed and pushed up so she was sitting. "I know. I tried to resist at first as well."

Cosmos flashed her an infectious grin. "Yeah, but I'm just so irresistible you didn't stand a chance," he teased, picking up her hand and pressing a hot kiss in the center of it.

Terra's laughter echoed over the small meadow, drawing his mother and Lal's attention. Ava Raines blushed as Lal grabbed her free hand with one hand while he slid a wildflower into the soft brown curls of her hair. He refused to let her go when she tried to pull away, drawing another blush from her as he pulled her instead toward them.

"Lord Raines," Lal greeted Cosmos with a small bow.

"How many times do I have to tell you to call me Cosmos, Lal?" Cosmos grinned. "All that Lord stuff is too much of a mouthful, especially among family."

"Cosmos," his mother admonished shyly. "Lal is going to stay for dinner with us. Tilly and Angus will be back from visiting with Hannah and Tansy. Tink is coming as well as she and her mom are working on a new generator concept and Angus wants to finish the last bit of proofing on his latest novel."

"That sounds great," Cosmos grinned. "What's the news at the palace, Lal? RITA2 has been busy with DAR working on a new defense system for the fortress which has been turned into a training facility from what I've heard."

"Yes," Lal said, shifting uneasily. "I have to admit she scares me at times. She walks around the palace all the time disappearing and reappearing through walls. She has half of the new warriors at the palace trying to follow her! I mean, have you seen her? Her figure is

...," he blushed when he saw Ava's raised eyebrow. "Yes, well, RITA2 has been a bit busy."

"What about Garrett and Rico?" Cosmos asked quietly, worried he had only heard from the men once since they reappeared a couple of months ago.

Garrett had shown up first. He and Darain's MFV had crashed during a massive storm. They had lost contact with Rico during the storm and had no way of contacting him as the MFV had been damaged beyond repair. It had been a harried few months as they fought their way across the vast Northern tundra before finally reaching Hendrik's Clan.

Rico had been torn between searching for his friend or saving his mate. The skimmer he was following had crashed during the same storm, only in the mountains further east. The MFV had been badly damaged as the skimmer had opened fire on it and the power drained. It had taken months for Rico and Vita to finally repair the MFV using parts from the crashed skimmer.

Since their return, both men had volunteered to go on missions. Rico was heading to another star system with Bullet, the Southern Clan leader on a Prime trade mission. Garrett had returned to Earth with Hendrik. Neither man had gone alone thanks to their time here on Baade.

"Bullet wanted me to tell you that a certain dark-haired Latino woman was in danger of being sold as soon as he reached the first port if she didn't quit giving him a hard time," Lal said with a grin. "I guess Rico's sister is giving him trouble from what Lan says."

Cosmos laughed as he thought of Maria and her tenacity. He felt almost as sorry for Bullet as he did for Core. Avery had disappeared shortly after she collected her 'bonus' a little over a month ago. It had taken a while to 'clean' up Avilov's mess. She had been working closely with a special task force the President had formed. Only a few of his cabinet members and high ranking military officers were aware of the on-going visits from another world.

When she returned to work, she had refused to discuss what happened. He hadn't talked to her since her return, but he suspected she might have bitten off more than she expected. She had immediately signed on for another mission.

He didn't go on missions anymore since Hong Kong. His sole mission in life was making sure Terra was safe and happy. They had been busy the last couple of months anyway with trying to see if the mating serum that they had developed worked. He had to admit, that was one mission that he didn't mind participating in.

I enjoyed it too, and it was very successful, she murmured silently, threading her fingers through his and resting it on her swollen belly.

Do you think your father is disappointed that you are only expecting one baby? He asked.

If he is, then he can have the other one, she growled softly. *I have been there through the births of Tink, Hannah, and Tansy's babies. Their mates know what it is like. Tansy made Mak go through the entire thing with her. He still looks at her in awe when he holds one of the twins. He swears he cannot figure out how something so large can come out of something so small. None of them want to have any more for a while after Tilly made them sit through that video on childbirth! You heard mother had to revive father after he passed out in the middle of it!*

He chuckled as he remembered Tilly, Angus, and Tresa laughing one night after dinner about it. Teriff had denied it was because of the film, but when Tilly asked if he would like to watch another one, he suddenly remembered that he and Tresa were needed elsewhere. He had overheard Tresa telling Terra that he had begged for her forgiveness for putting her through that five times. He swore he would spend the rest of his life making it up to her.

Cosmos leaned his chin on Terra's shoulder, enjoying holding her close as he listened to Lal tell them more about what was happening at the palace. He already knew most of it thanks to RITA and RITA2. Nothing much got by those two.

He knew that Teriff was upset because Derik kept periodically disappearing through the Gateway. Teriff threatened that if RITA2 didn't quit opening a portal for Derik, he was going to disable DAR for a month. All RITA and her sis would tell him was that Derik said he was looking for something. Cosmos suspected it was more of a someone and he had a feeling that it was a girl with a penchant for hacking into computers. He knew Avery was looking for Runt as well since she disappeared almost a year ago from his warehouse.

"Cosmos, how long are you staying this time?" Ava Raines asked after a while.

Cosmos looked down at Terra with a sigh of regret. "We are working on several big projects right now, mom. We can only stay a few days, but we'll be popping back and forth. You can always come and stay with us at the warehouse," he said.

"No!" Lal growled out, possessively pulling Ava closer to him. "She will remain here."

"I declare," Ava said, glaring up at the huge warrior. "I can come and go as I please, thank you very much!"

Cosmos bit back a smile as he watched his normally placid mother turn and glare up at the man towering over her slightly plump frame. She was beginning to blossom again. Tilly and Angus both said they had seen a difference since his mom had met the huge warrior almost four months ago.

"You are mine, Ava Raines," Lal growled out in a low voice. "I cannot protect you on your world."

Ava's eyes widened when she saw the silver flames burning deep in his eyes. Her hand rose to cover her heart that was fluttering as if she had just run a mile. Her hand fell to her side when he suddenly reached out and touched her cheek with the tips of his fingers.

"You are my bond mate," he said quietly. "I will wait for you until you are ready. All I ask is that you stay here where I can see and protect you."

"I …," she turned to look at Cosmos, her eyes pleading. "I think it would be better if I stay here… for a little while."

"I think that is a wonderful idea, mom," Cosmos said. "I think that dad would feel better if you were to stay here too."

Ava looked at her son, tears glistening in her eyes as she thought about her late husband. "Do you really think so?" She asked in a voice filled with hope.

"I know so," Cosmos responded gently. "He wouldn't want you to be alone. He would want you to live life to the fullest."

Ava's lips trembled for a moment before a small smile blossomed and her whole face glowed. She looked up at Lal again and this time he saw the hope, curiosity, and – something else shining in the depths of her beautiful brown eyes. He held his hand out, waiting to see if she was ready to finally take the first step toward healing and accepting him. His expression softened as she tentatively reached out and placed her trembling hand in his.

"We'll see you both at dinner," Lal said respectfully.

"Or not," Ava said under her breath as Lal pulled her away toward a small group of woods.

Terra grinned as she watched Lal help Ava over a small dip in the trail away from the house. She leaned back against Cosmos and let out a tired sigh. She was suddenly very sleepy. That was not uncommon since she became pregnant.

"Sleepy again?" Cosmos asked, drawing her down beside him in the tall grass. "I know something that will help you sleep better," he whispered, sliding his hand over her fuller breast.

Terra rolled her eyes. "We are out in the middle of a field. Someone might see us," she chuckled.

"No one is going to see us," Cosmos murmured persuasively right before a large shadow covered them.

"I owe you an apple pie, J'kar. You were right. They are getting frisky in the grass," Tilly sighed.

"I told you, Tilly," J'kar said with a grin. "It is the chemicals. I could not keep my hands off Tink when she was pregnant."

Cosmos groaned as he buried his face in Terra's neck. "Please tell me the whole family isn't standing there watching us."

Terra peeked over Cosmos' shoulder. Sure enough, everyone except for Ava and Lal were standing over them grinning. She giggled when Cosmos let out a muffled curse when he heard the squeals of the babies. Turning her head, she brushed a kiss against his ear.

"They are all there," she whispered. "Including…"

"Hi Cosmos! Guess what I can do now?" RITA said cheerfully. "I thought I'd come visit my sis for a while!"

*To be continued with **Merrick's Maiden**…*

Preview of *Merrick's Maiden*

(Cosmos' Gateway: Book 5)

Synopsis

Merrick Ta'Duran is the powerful leader of the Eastern Mountain Clan on the Prime world of Baade. His people, known as the Ghosts of the Forests, live high in the Eastern mountains. Merrick feels the weight of responsibility as the males within his clan become desperate to find mates among the few remaining females. When word comes that a new species has been discovered, he knows he must do what is right for his people - even if it means traveling to a strange, alien realm to do it.

Merrick's world changes when he is injured and captured by a ruthless group of humans. Drugged and held against his will, he is the subject of experiments and testing as the humans try to discover where he came from and duplicate his strength and ability to heal quickly. After months of captivity, he fears his life will end on the strange world until one chance encounter gives him hope.

Addie Banks' world has been one of silence since a devastating illness when she was sixteen. Determined to stand on her own two feet, she goes to school during the day and works at night to put herself through college. Her life unexpectedly changes when she stumbles across something she wasn't supposed to see while at work. Now, she hears a voice in her head - and it is driving her crazy. Her only hope for peace is to help the creature talking to her escape from the men holding him.

Merrick knows the female who helps him is his bond mate. She may deny it. She may fight it. She may even try to run from it, but it won't matter. She is his and he will do everything he can to convince her, hold her, even kidnap her if that is what it takes to make her realize that they belong together.

Will Addie hear the love and longing in Merrick's voice? Can she trust and accept the new life he has to offer? Or, will a ruthless killer silence him before she gets a chance?

Characters' Relationships:

Teriff, Prime Leader of Baade – **mated to** Tresa:
four sons, J'kar, Borj, Mak, and Derik and one
daughter, Terra
Angus and Tilly Bell, humans – **married**:
three daughters, Hannah, Tansy and Tink

Warriors of Baade:

J'kar 'Tag Krell Manok **mated to** Jasmine 'Tinker' Bell:
twin daughters, Wendy and Tessa
Borj 'Tag Krell Manok **mated to** Hannah Bell: twin boy
& girl, Sky and Ocean
Mak 'Tag Krell Manok **mated to** Tansy Bell: twin
daughters, Sonya and Mackenzie
Terra 'Tag Krell Manok **mated to** Cosmos Raines
Derik 'Tag Krell Manok **mated to** Runt

Members of Cosmos' security team:

Garrett	Avery
Trudy	Rose
Rico	Maria

Prime Warriors of Bade:

Merrick, Eastern Clan Leader, **mated to** Addie
Core **mated to** Avery
Lan **mated to** Natasha
Brock **mated to** Helene
Lal **mated to** Ava Raines
Gant, Western Plains Clan Leader
Brawn, Desert Clan Leader

Bullet, Southern Clan Leader, **mated to** Maria
Hendrik, Northern Clan Leader

RITA (Earth) **zapped by** FRED
RITA2 (Baade) **zapped by** DAR

If you loved this story by me (S.E. Smith) please leave
a review. You can also take a look at additional books
and sign up for my newsletter at **http://sesmithfl.com**
to hear about my latest releases or keep in touch using
the following links:

Website: http://sesmithfl.com
Newsletter: http://sesmithfl.com/?s=newsletter
Facebook: https://www.facebook.com/se.smith.5
Twitter: https://twitter.com/sesmithfl
Pinterest: http://www.pinterest.com/sesmithfl/
Blog: http://sesmithfl.com/blog/
Forum: http://www.sesmithromance.com/forum/

Excerpts of S.E. Smith Books

If you would like to read more S.E. Smith stories, she
recommends Hunter's Claim, the first in her Alliance
series. Or if you prefer a Paranormal or Western with
a twist, you can check out Lily's Cowboys or Indiana
Wild…

Additional Books by S.E. Smith

Short Stories and Novellas

(Dragon Lords of Valdier: Book 3)
Ambushing Ariel
(Dragon Lords of Valdier: Book 4)
Cornering Carmen
(Dragon Lords of Valdier: Book 5)
Paul's Pursuit
(Dragon Lords of Valdier: Book 6)
Twin Dragons
(Dragon Lords of Valdier: Book 7)
Jaguin's Love
(Dragon Lords of Valdier: Book 8)
The Old Dragon of the Mountain's Christmas
(Dragon Lords of Valdier: Book 9)

Lords of Kassis Series

River's Run
(Lords of Kassis: Book 1)
Star's Storm
(Lords of Kassis: Book 2)
Jo's Journey
(Lords of Kassis: Book 3)
Ristéard's Unwilling Empress
(Lords of Kassis: Book 4)

Magic, New Mexico Series

Touch of Frost
(Magic, New Mexico Book 1)
Taking on Tory
(Magic, New Mexico Book 2)

Sarafin Warriors

Choosing Riley
(Sarafin Warriors: Book 1)
Viper's Defiant Mate
(Sarafin Warriors Book 2)

The Alliance Series

Hunter's Claim
> (The Alliance: Book 1)

Razor's Traitorous Heart
> (The Alliance: Book 2)

Dagger's Hope
> (The Alliance: Book 3)

Challenging Saber
> (The Alliance: Book 4)

Zion Warriors Series

Gracie's Touch
> (Zion Warriors: Book 1)

Krac's Firebrand
> (Zion Warriors: Book 2)

Paranormal and Time Travel Novels

Spirit Pass Series

Indiana Wild
> (Spirit Pass: Book 1)

Spirit Warrior
> (Spirit Pass Book 2)

Second Chance Series

Lily's Cowboys
> (Second Chance: Book 1)

Touching Rune
> (Second Chance: Book 2)

Young Adult Novels

Breaking Free Series

Voyage of the Defiance
> (Breaking Free: Book 1)

Recommended Reading Order Lists:

http://sesmithfl.com/reading-list-by-events/
http://sesmithfl.com/reading-list-by-series/

About S.E. Smith

S.E. Smith is a *New York Times, USA TODAY, International, and Award-Winning* Bestselling author of science fiction, fantasy, paranormal, and contemporary works for adults, young adults, and children. She enjoys writing a wide variety of genres that pull her readers into worlds that take them away.